About the author

CW01081591

David Fuller is an FA-q
currently coaches a you
He has worked as a jour............... ....,
during which time he has written for numerous
publications on a variety of different subjects. David
lives in Newhaven, East Sussex with his wife, two
sons and cat Merry.

Other books by David Fuller

Alfie Jones series
Alfie Jones and a change of fortune
Alfie Jones and a test of character
Alfie Jones and the missing link
Alfie Jones and an uncertain future
Alfie Jones and the big decision

Other books
A Footballer's Christmas Carol
Split Loyalties *

* Currently only available on Kindle

To Asiyah

ⵣ

RDF Publishing
3 Courtlands Mews, Church Hill, Newhaven,
East Sussex,
BN9 9LU

Alfie Jones and a Crisis of Confidence
A RDF Publishing book

First published in Great Britain by RDF Publishing in 2018
Printed and bound in Great Britain by Clays Ltd, Elcograf S.p.A.

1
Text copyright © David Fuller
Images courtesy of Stuart Liddiard

ISBN 978·0·9570339·6·2

For more exclusive Alfie Jones content, visit:
www.alfie-jones.co.uk

ALFIE JONES AND A CRISIS OF CONFIDENCE

DAVID FULLER

Illustrated by
Stuart Liddiard

www.alfie-jones.co.uk

Sunday

Chapter one

The room was silent. You could have heard a pin drop.

Nine boys sat rooted to benches. Motionless. None of them made eye contact. None of them made a sound.

Finally, after what seemed like an eternity, the silence was broken by the creak of a door opening. Instantly, Alfie Jones' eyes, along with those belonging to the other eight boys in the room, turned towards the sound.

A boy roughly the same age as those seated on the benches stepped through the office door. Then slammed it shut behind him. There was no need for anyone to ask how he had fared.

The look on his face said it all.

Rejected.

The dejected teenager shuffled through the room.

Not one of his, now former, Norton Town Under 13s teammates said a word. Swiftly, the remaining boys all resumed staring at the same floor, wall or ceiling space that they had been studying so intently prior to the door being opened. Not one of them knew what to say. There was nothing to say.

Even after he had left the changing room, the nine boys remained frozen in their seats. As still as statues.

They stayed that way for a good few minutes, stirring only when the office door finally re-opened. Seconds later, Matty Simmons entered the changing room.

Matty was the Head Coach of the Norton Town Under 13s Academy team. He was usually a supremely confident, composed individual. Today, though, even he looked stressed and anxious.

There was a good reason for this. He felt stressed and anxious.

This was by far the worst part of Matty's job. He loved delivering coaching sessions, adored match days (especially when his team won), and didn't even mind handing out a good old fashioned telling off when he felt his players deserved it.

But having to look into a young boy's eyes as he told them that they weren't going to be kept on at Norton Town for another season... well, that was something he would never get used to. Ever.

Nevertheless, it was something he had to do. Every year. It was part of his job.

At the end of every season, Matty, along with his coaching team, would get together to assess the progress of the 18 players in their squad.

They discussed who had improved sufficiently and, more importantly, who hadn't. They predicted whether it was likely that a certain player would develop any further or whether they felt they had reached their very top level. They talked at great length about which of the boys had a good attitude and were willing to learn and which ones were not. They also considered whether there were any better players available in the local area.

After debating each of these points over many hours, days and sometimes even weeks, the coaches would then make two lists. On one list went the names of the boys they would be keeping for another year. On the other went the names of those they were letting go.

All 18 players were then invited to Norton Town's East Side Park training complex to be told of their fate. Although he hated delivering bad news, Matty strongly believed in meeting each player face to face. He wanted to at least attempt to let down those who had been unsuccessful as gently as possible.

So far today, seven boys had been let go. Only two had been retained.

Matty craned his neck, searching for the next boy on his list. For a moment, Alfie was convinced his coach's gaze had settled on him. However, just as he thought he was about to be called, Matty focused on the boy sitting to his right.

"Giorgio," Matty said, in an even tone that betrayed no hint of what the outcome of their discussion would be. "In you come."

Giorgio Rossi shifted uncomfortably. For a moment, Alfie thought his friend was not going to be able to stand. He even wondered whether he was going to be sick. Right there, on the floor beside him.

Eventually, though, Giorgio gathered the strength to stand and unsteadily made his way towards Matty's office.

Once their teammate had entered the room, the eight remaining boys all let out a sharp intake of breath. Then went back to their silent staring.

Alfie had wanted to wish Giorgio good luck. In the 18 months that he had been in Norton Town's Academy, he had grown closer to Giorgio than he had to any of his other teammates. They had joined the Academy at the same time and had just finished their first full season with Norton.

But he had been unable to get so much as a word out. He had, instead, tried to nod his head in an encouraging manner. He had not even managed to do this.

He was simply too nervous to do anything. Like all the other boys, he just sat there, lost in his own thoughts. Nervously waiting for his turn to enter the office. Hoping, beyond hope, that when the time came, the news he received would be good. He dared not think about how he would react otherwise.

Seconds turned to minutes. The office door remained closed. For the umpteenth time that day, Alfie went over the past season in his mind. Had you asked him a few hours earlier, he would have told you that the season had gone well. He had started every game apart from two, scored a respectable six goals and provided more assists than any other player in the squad.

However, the more Alfie replayed the season to himself, the more he started to dwell on the few errors he had made.

Could he have made more tackles? Should he have been braver when in possession of the ball? Did he take the safe option too many times? Were six goals enough for an attacking wide midfielder?

The waiting was giving him too much time to think. It was torture.

Eventually, the office door reopened. Giorgio Rossi practically skipped through it. A beaming smile lit up his face. There could be little doubt that he had just become the third player to be kept on for the coming season.

Alfie was delighted for this friend. He was also a little jealous. Giorgio had received the exact news he himself wanted to hear. Alfie, though, was still waiting. Still unsure as to whether he'd be leaving the office elated or deflated.

As it turned out, he wouldn't have to wait much longer for an answer. Moments later, Matty reappeared in the changing room, looked directly at him and said the words he'd been eagerly anticipating and dreading in equal measure.

"In you come then, Alfie. It's your turn."

Chapter two

Matty's office was an extremely small, box-shaped room. The walls, painted in Norton Town's colours of black and white, were covered by whiteboards, year planners and tactics charts.

The office was dominated by a large desk in the centre of the room. On it was a laptop computer, numerous tablet devices, two mobile phones and four neatly stacked piles of paper. Alfie could see nothing that gave any hint as to what the outcome of the coming discussion would be.

Behind the desk were two comfy looking leather chairs. Matty settled himself in one. In the other sat Noel Forint. The scout who had first spotted Alfie playing for the Kingsway Colts Under 11s.

Matty invited Alfie to sit in the less cosy looking hard-backed chair on the opposite side of the desk.

"So, Alfie," the coach began once the boy had taken his seat. "How do you think you've done this season?"

The question took Alfie by surprise. He hadn't expected to be asked anything. He hadn't really known what to expect.

"Erm..."he stuttered, after a brief pause. "All right, I suppose. I mean, I guess I could have scored a few more goals. Maybe sometimes I could keep the ball for a bit longer and look to pass forwards more, rather than sideways or backwards. I know I'm not the best tackler in the world, and..."

Alfie's answer was halted by the sound of hearty laughter. It was Noel.

"Lad, can I stop you there for a moment?" the scout began, once he had finished chuckling. "Wouldn't it make more sense to point out all the things that you're good at first, rather than the things you consider to be your weaknesses? Maybe myself or Matty hadn't noticed some of the things you were saying. We will now."

Alfie gulped, fearful that he had made a grave error.

"Now, lad," Noel continued, giving the teenager a warm, encouraging smile. "Tell us all about the things that you're good at."

The boy thought for a moment. He cleared his throat, then began to speak. "Well, I have set up more goals than any other player in the squad this season. I very rarely give possession away. I can't remember off the top of my head making any errors that led to the other team scoring a goal. I think I'm a hard worker. I always do my best at training. I'm willing to learn. And, erm... I'm sure there are some other things that I'm good at, too."

"That's better, lad," Noel said. He winked at Alfie. The teenager smiled.

Matty leaned back in his chair and placed both hands behind his head. He looked thoughtful but didn't say a word.

As the silence dragged on, Alfie began wondering whether the coach was waiting for him to say more. He desperately started thinking of some other strengths he could list. Then Matty looked at him and began to talk.

"I would agree with every single one of those positive points," he said. "You're certainly one of the hardest

workers and most dedicated trainers
in the team. In fact, I can't remember
coaching many boys your age who have
the same desire to succeed that you do. I
would also disagree with what you were
saying about not being brave enough
in possession. I think, over the past 18
months, you have become an increasingly
intelligent player. There's a time to go
forward and a time to keep the ball. I
would say that seven times out of ten you
choose the right option. It's one of the
reasons you make so many assists."

Understandably, Alfie was encouraged
by what he was hearing.

However, he had a nagging feeling that

there was a 'but' coming.

He was right.

"But," Matty continued. "The fact that, as Noel pointed out, you were so willing to list your flaws first, is one of the major concerns that I have about you. You lack confidence in your own ability."

Suddenly, Alfie wasn't too keen on the direction this conversation was taking.

"Now, I'm not saying you need to be cocky and arrogant," Matty carried on. "But a little bit more self-belief certainly wouldn't go amiss. For example, take the way you talk about your friends who play for Kingsway United..."

Two of Alfie's closest friends, Billy Morris and Hayden Whitlock, both played for the United Academy. Another friend, Reuben Ryan, was also there. Alfie had once dreamed of playing for the Kingsway United Academy himself. It was the team he supported. However, he had ultimately decided to join Norton Town's Academy, despite the fact United had shown an interest in signing him.

"... It's like you believe they're so much better than you. That when you play for the school team together you don't deserve to be on the same pitch as them. You can't have this attitude when you play. Not if you want to make it at the very highest level," the coach warned. "You are every bit as good as they are. You need to believe that in here." The coach tapped the side of his head.

Reluctantly, Alfie had to admit that what Matty was saying was true. Whenever he played alongside Hayden, Billy or Reuben for the Tideway Secondary School team he would often marvel at how good his three teammates were.

Matty took a deep breath. Alfie could sense that the coach was just about to reveal his decision. He unconsciously closed his eyes. He had no idea what the verdict would be.

"That's why, Alfie..." The teenager didn't like the soothing tone the adult's voice had suddenly taken. Was Matty preparing to let him down gently? "... when you come back next season, I want to see a new, more confident Alfie Jones. Find that self-belief, and keep working hard. Improve as much as you have this year, and I really believe you have got a great future ahead of you."

It took a moment for the coach's words to sink in.

"You mean?" Alfie began, his blue eyes

opening as wide as they would go. "I'm being kept on!"

"Of course you are, lad," Noel answered. He was grinning arguably as much as Alfie was. "Congratulations. You deserve it."

The next few minutes passed like a dream. Alfie was vaguely aware of Matty and Noel asking him to keep as level headed as possible until he got out of the changing rooms. This, they explained, was to spare the feelings of the boys who wouldn't be retained. Other than that, he couldn't have told you anything else they said to him. He was in a world of his own.

A few minutes later, Alfie found himself in the car park of the Norton Town training complex. He had no recollection of how he got there. His head was spinning. He could have floated out of the building for all he knew. He certainly felt like he was flying at that particular moment. Realising there was no one else around, he jumped as high as he could and punched the air. He then let out an excited, ear-piercing scream of delight.

Calming down, he glanced at his watch to check the time. It was 13:20. His parents had said they would pick him up at 14:00.

He took his mobile phone out of his
pocket and saw that he had a message
from Daisy Saunders asking him how he
had got on.

Daisy had been Alfie's girlfriend for
over a year. If truth be told, he still found
it odd to have a girlfriend. Especially
one that had no real interest in football.
In fact, they didn't have that much in
common at all. Nevertheless, they got on
fabulously well together and barely ever
argued.

Alfie was just about to reply with
the good news when, all of a sudden,
something strange happened. His phone
began making a weird noise. One that it
had never made before.

Yet the sound his phone was making
was one that Alfie recognised only too
well.

Chapter three

T-ting-a-ching. T-ting-a-ching. T-ting-a-ching.
The tinkling sound of wind chimes chiming was unmistakable to Alfie. It was one he had heard many times before. More often than not, the familiar rhythmic dinging of wind chimes meant only one thing. Madam Zola was nearby.

Madam Zola was a fortune teller who Alfie had first met at a fun-fair when he was just nine years old. During that meeting, she had told the young boy that it was his destiny to one day become a professional footballer. Providing he listened to any advice that she gave him.

In the years that had followed, Madam Zola had appeared to Alfie on a handful of occasions. These appearances would, more often than not, be preceded by the sound of wind chimes.

Therefore, it was no real surprise when, just a few seconds after the strange chiming had begun, the fortune teller's face suddenly appeared on Alfie's phone screen. The chiming instantly stopped. He hadn't had to touch anything.

The fortune teller still looked exactly the same as she had the first time they had met. Even now, she reminded Alfie of a friendly looking witch. She had a long thin face, dominated by a crooked nose. Instead of a witch's hat, though, her flowing grey hair was, as ever, covered by a purple and green headscarf. Strangely, despite having known her for over four years, Alfie didn't really think she had aged so much as a day in this time. Then again, she had looked extremely old to start with. Maybe extremely old people just aged at a slower rate, the boy considered to himself.

"Alfie! How lovely it is to see you," Madam Zola exclaimed. Her brown eyes positively twinkled, so happy was she to be talking to him. "You must be absolutely delighted to have been kept on at the Academy for another season. Congratulations!"

Although Alfie had not yet told anyone

about being kept on at the Norton Town Academy, he wasn't in the least bit surprised to discover that Madam Zola already knew that he had been. The elderly fortune teller always seemed to know everything about him. Nor was he overly shocked to find himself staring at her through his phone screen. Over the years, Madam Zola had popped up in a number of bizarre places. Including on his parents' TV screen.

"Yeah, it's great. I'm really happy," he replied. "I was so nervous, though. Waiting to find out if I was going to make it through to the under 14s. There was a moment when I really thought they were going to say no."

"What? Of course they weren't going to say no," Madam Zola cried. "Why on earth would they have said no to you? From what I hear you've been playing and training really well. You're one of the team's best players and hardest workers. You really need to have more confidence in yourself, young man," the fortune teller admonished.

Alfie smiled. "That's exactly what Matty Simmons, the coach, told me."

"Yes, I know very well that's what he said," Madam Zola answered, matter of factly. "Of course I knew that. I know everything. Remember?"

The teenager laughed. "I remember."

"Anyway, this is just a very quick call to say well done," Madam Zola continued. "I'm a bit pressed for time, you see." She glanced down at her wrist as if to check the time. She wasn't actually wearing a watch, but details like this never seemed to matter to her. "Oh my word. Is that the time already?" she said more to herself than to Alfie. "I really must get going."

The fortune teller removed her eyes from her bare wrist and looked straight ahead once again. A serious expression worked its way across her face. "Just remember, while it's good to be confident, do not end up becoming boastful and big headed," she warned. "Think about other people's feelings at all times. Remember, not everyone will have heard good news today. There will be some whose dreams have been shattered. The last thing they need is you rubbing it in."

The boy was just about to promise Madam Zola that he would remain humble, but before he could, the vision of the fortune teller disappeared from his screen just as quickly as it had appeared.

He was left looking at the message from

19

Daisy that he had just been about to reply to.

A thought crossed his mind. He tapped a few times at his phone screen and brought up a list of the most recent people to have called him. According to the list, Daisy was the last person who had phoned him. There was no mention of Madam Zola, or any numbers he didn't recognise, having contacted him. In truth, Alfie hadn't for one second thought there would be. But he figured it was worth checking. Just in case.

Alfie messaged his response to Daisy, then phoned his parents to see if they were close enough to pick him up a little earlier than they had originally agreed. He was in luck. Mr and Mrs Jones had just finished shopping in Norton Town Centre and were already on their way to him. They should be no more than ten minutes, his Mum told him once she had finished excitably screaming upon hearing her son's good news.

As he waited for them to arrive, Alfie considered the fortune teller's warning. Matty Simmons and Noel Forint had already warned him about the importance of staying level headed. He had absolutely no intention whatsoever

of boasting to others about his success.
Especially to those who had not been
lucky enough to be retained for the under
14s squad.

Anyway, aside from Giorgio, he didn't
often speak to any of his Norton Town
teammates outside of the academy. And,
judging by Giorgio's reaction when he had
left Matty's office, Alfie was fairly certain
his friend had also been retained.

It was unlikely he would see any of
those who had been let go ever again.
Therefore, the chances of him hurting
any of his former teammates feelings
were slim. For once this was a warning
that Madam Zola did not really need to
have given him.

Or so he thought.

Monday

Chapter four

It was inside the school common room the following morning that Alfie realised the fortune teller had not been referring to his former Norton Town teammates.

When he had first heard the news, he'd refused to believe it. He assumed Hayden had been joking. But then he spoke to Reuben, who told Alfie the exact same thing.

Momentarily he thought that both friends were pulling his leg. The solemn expressions on both their faces confirmed that they weren't.

Billy had been let go from the Kingsway United Academy. Hayden and Reuben had been retained.

Alfie was shocked. Not at Hayden and Reuben being kept on. That came as no surprise to him at all. But he simply could not believe that his best friend had been released. He could only begin to imagine how devastated Billy must be feeling.

Suddenly, Alfie felt a surge of guilt flow through him. He had sent Billy a text message the previous evening, letting him know that he had been retained by Norton. At the time, he had been annoyed that Billy had failed to respond. Now he understood why he hadn't.

The feeling of guilt was quickly replaced by one of concern. For himself. Did this mean he had failed to properly heed Madam Zola's warning? Surely the innocent text he had sent his best friend could not be classed as boasting. Could it? He certainly hadn't meant for the message to be insensitive.

Anger then overtook concern. Surely Madam Zola would have known that Billy was going to be let go by United. Why couldn't she have just told him this when he had spoken to her on the phone? It was obvious that Billy would have been among the first people he would tell his good news to.

The fortune teller really did infuriate him sometimes!

Quickly realising that he was being selfish by worrying about himself instead of Billy, Alfie attempted to push his own feelings aside for the time being.

Carefully, he studied the faces of the two boys standing in front of him. "You are being serious, aren't you?" he inquired. "This isn't a joke? One of those where you say he hasn't been kept on, but really he has."

"I promise we're telling the truth, Alfie," Hayden replied.

"It's true," Reuben insisted.

"But why would Jimmy let him go?" Alfie wondered aloud.

Jimmy Grimshaw was the Head of Youth Development at Kingsway United. He had been both Alfie and Billy's first ever football coach back when they played for the Kingsway Colts Under 9s. Alfie had always been extremely close to the elderly coach and could hardly believe that Jimmy would snatch Billy's dream of one day playing for United away from him.

Hayden shrugged his shoulders. "I don't know. To be honest, Jimmy tends to deal with the younger age groups these days. He doesn't come and watch us that much anymore. He doesn't attend our training sessions very often, either. It might not have been his decision."

"But he's the Head of Youth Development," Alfie raged. "It's obviously his decision."

Again, Hayden shrugged his shoulders. "I suppose he can only go by what the other coaches tell him. And if they say he's not good enough, then..."

"Of course he's good enough," Alfie snapped. "How can you say that he's not good enough? He's supposed to be your friend."

"Hey, don't take it out on me," Hayden answered defensively. "I do think he's good enough. We were both as shocked as you are." He gestured towards Reuben. "I'm just saying that it probably wasn't only Jimmy's decision. That's all."

"Sorry H," Alfie said, well aware that Hayden would also be disappointed for their friend. "It's just a huge shock. Billy must be absolutely gutted."

Hayden and Reuben both nodded their agreement. "I tried to talk to Billy yesterday after I heard the news," Reuben stated. "But he didn't want to speak to me. To anyone in fact. I called round for him on the way to school this morning. He's not coming in. His Dad told me that he's barely been out of his bedroom since he got home yesterday."

"I'm not surprised. I think I would be the same," Alfie said. He thought back to how nervous he had felt as he waited in the changing room to discover whether or not he was going to be retained. Words could not begin to have described how despondent he would have been had he not received the desired outcome.

Although he was supposed to be going to the cinema with Daisy after school, Alfie decided there and then that he would cancel his plans and go and see Billy instead. Daisy would understand. Probably.

He didn't have a clue what he would actually say to him, but Billy was his best friend. He had to at least try to cheer him up.

He also wanted to make sure that Billy realised his text message the previous evening had not been boastful, and that he hadn't meant it to be insensitive.

***

Sitting in the school canteen later that day, Jasper Johnson smiled wickedly to himself. He had just heard Billy's unfortunate news. Not that Jasper thought it was unfortunate. Not even a tiny little bit.

He wasn't even that surprised by the news. After all, he himself – the great Jasper Johnson – had also once been let go by the Kingsway United Academy. And in his misguided mind, he was a far better football player than Billy.

In truth, Jasper did not really give two hoots as to whether Billy was a member of the Kingsway United Academy or not. Yet upon hearing the news he instantly sensed an opportunity.

An opportunity to finally get one over on his arch rival, Alfie Jones.

Jasper had never liked Alfie. Not from the very first moment he had met him. He couldn't have told you why. He just didn't. That said, Jasper didn't like anyone very much.

It was being beaten by Alfie in a one-on-one football match back when they were only nine years old that had really angered Jasper. Even now, more than four years later, the memory of Alfie celebrating his flukey victory was enough to bring an angry flush of crimson to his face. He still all too painfully recalled the humiliation he felt at losing to the little muppet. Not to mention the disappointment in his own Dad's eyes as he trudged off the pitch a loser.

For years, Jasper had tried, and failed, to take his revenge on Alfie. But this time he knew things would be different. This time he knew he could take away the only thing that meant more to Alfie Jones than football.

Chapter five

"Billy, Alfie's here to see you," Mr Morris called up the stairs.

There was no reply.

Billy's Dad sighed. "He's hardly said a word since yesterday," he moaned to Alfie. "I've never seen him like this. Go on up. But don't take it personally if he doesn't say much. He's taken what happened with United really badly."

Sluggishly, Alfie climbed the stairs. He was still trying to work out exactly what he was going to say to his friend. What could he possibly say that would make him feel any better?

He had tried putting himself in Billy's position. Was there anything anyone could have said to him that would have made him feel better if he'd been let go by

Norton? He seriously doubted it.

Arriving at Billy's closed bedroom door, Alfie took a deep breath, then knocked three times. No response.

"Billy, it's Alfie," he called gently. For a moment there was nothing but silence. Then, very faintly, Alfie was certain he heard his friend grunt.

Taking this as an invitation to enter the room, Alfie took yet another deep breath, placed his left hand on the handle and slowly opened the door.

Billy was sitting on the edge of his bed, blasting aliens on his X·Box. He didn't acknowledge Alfie's presence. Still unsure as how best to proceed with a conversation, Alfie merely sat down at the other end of the bed and watched his friend take his anger out on strange looking space creatures.

The uncomfortable silence dragged on. Billy just continued staring sullenly at his TV, hammering at the buttons on his controller. Alfie wasn't sure whether the other boy even knew he was there or not.

Glancing around the room, it became instantly apparent at just how upset his best mate was.

The latest Kingsway United squad poster had been ripped from the wall

above the radiator. A seasonally upd:
version of this poster had occupied th
exact spot for as long as Alfie had known
Billy. Now, though, the only evidence
that anything had ever been there were
four tiny rips on the wall and the slightly
faded paintwork. Framed pictures of Billy
proudly wearing his Kingsway United kit
had also been removed, leaving nothing
but a row of uncovered hooks fixed to the
wall opposite.

Noticing a black bin bag over by the
waste paper bin in the far corner of the
room, Alfie decided to investigate. He
doubted Billy would even notice what he
was doing.

Peering into the bag, Alfie could hardly
believe what he saw. It was crammed
full of football gear. There were football
shirts, tracksuits, football boots, shin-
pads, magazines... even a copy of the
latest FIFA game. Momentarily, Alfie
was torn. He didn't have the latest FIFA
yet. He had wanted it for ages. If Billy
was throwing his copy away, maybe he
should ask if he could have it? At least it
would be a way of getting a conversation
started.

Sensibly deciding that this would
probably not be the best way to go about

doing so, Alfie let go of the bag and returned to his position on the bed.

Feeling the ripple on the mattress as his friend plonked back down, Billy quickly glanced over his shoulder, then resumed staring at the screen in front of him. "Take whatever you want from there," he mumbled. "I don't need it anymore."

Part of Alfie wanted to rush over to the bag and grab the game before Billy changed his mind. Instead, he merely replied, "Don't be silly. It's yours."

"Told you, don't need it anymore," Billy grouched. "I'm done with football."

"Look, Billy," Alfie began soothingly. "I know you're upset right now, but..."

Before he could say anything more, Billy paused his game, and turned to face Alfie. He raised his right palm to silence his friend. "Don't take this the wrong way, Alf," Billy said. "But you really don't have a clue how I'm feeling right now. I don't want to talk about this yet. Not with you. Not with anyone."

With that, he turned back to face the TV, unpaused his game and resumed his destructive mission. "Join in if you want," Billy continued after a short pause. The way he said it sounded more like a demand than an offer. "Spare controller

is up there," he added, nodding in the
direction of a shelf above Alfie's head.

As instructed, Alfie stood up, grabbed
the spare controller and joined his friend
in pulverising aliens. For a while neither
boy said a word. Both of them were
totally absorbed in the game.

Eventually, it was Billy who broke the
silence. "It's not fair," he whined.

It took a moment for Alfie to realise
what his buddy was talking about.
Billy was doing well on the game. Then
he realised he was talking about the
situation with Kingsway United.

"Loads of us were let go. It sucks!"

Alfie waited a short while before saying

anything. He wanted to see whether Billy would say more. When it became clear that he wouldn't, Alfie decided to ask the question he had been wanting to ask ever since he had heard the news.

"Did Jimmy say why you were being let go?" he asked tentatively, keeping his eyes fixed firmly on the TV screen.

Seconds passed. Billy didn't respond. He just kept tapping away at his controller, his face a mask of concentration as he attempted to overcome a particularly tricky extra-terrestrial. Alfie feared he had pushed too soon, prompting Billy to clam up again.

Then, having overcome the latest bad guy, Billy paused the game and slowly turned to face his best friend.

"He told me that because the first team has been promoted into the Championship, the club are changing the way they run their Academy."

"What does that mean?" Alfie asked.

Billy shrugged. "I'm not sure. Jimmy did try to explain it to me. He said something about the club wanting to attract more players from outside of the Kingsway area. He even mentioned bringing in boys from Spain and Italy and places like that. To be honest, I wasn't really listening.

As soon as he told me I was being let go..." Billy's voice quavered suddenly. Alfie could see tears starting to form in the corner of his friend's eyes. "... well, I couldn't concentrate."

Billy once again fell silent and refocussed on the computer game.

Another short period of silence followed before Alfie attempted to resume their conversation. "What you said earlier about being done with football. You didn't mean that, right? I mean, there are other teams you can play for and..."

Once again, Billy's raised palm halted Alfie's flow. "Right now, I've got no interest in playing football ever again. I've always dreamed of playing for United and if I can't do that, well... then what's the point?"

Before Alfie could respond, Billy continued speaking. "Now please, can we just not speak about football anymore. You're making me lose my concen... Oh rubbish!" Billy exclaimed angrily as, on the screen, his character was gobbled up by a fearsome looking foe.

"Sorry," Alfie offered guiltily. He didn't know whether he felt worse for pushing his friend to talk about something he clearly didn't want to talk about, or making him lose a life on the game. "Just one more thing, then I promise I'll never mention football ever again. Or at least not for the rest of the week. Promise, promise, promise."

Billy rolled his eyes. "Go on," he sighed.

"It's just..." Alfie began. "That message I sent you last night. About Norton Town. I wasn't boasting or anything. If I'd have known what had happened I never would have sent it. I'm really sorry."

Slowly, a small smile worked its way across Billy's lips. Then he did something that really surprised Alfie. He chuckled. Slightly. "Alf, don't be silly. You're the least boastful person I know. And I am happy for you. Sorry, I should have replied. It's just..." He paused, struggling to find the words to explain the way he was feeling.

"It's okay. I understand," Alfie reassured him. He was majorly relieved that Billy had not felt his message had been insensitive.

The two boys sat playing various, non-football, X-Box games for the next two hours. They barely spoke a word to each other in that time. Yet the silence was no longer uncomfortable. They were just totally absorbed in the games.

It was only when Alfie received a text
message from his Mum, asking him
where he was, that he realised just how
late it was getting. Bidding his friend
farewell, and promising not to talk to him
about football at school the next day, Alfie
left the house and began walking home.

He was about halfway there when his
phone beeped again.

'Give me a chance, I'm on my way,' the
teenager said to himself, thinking that
it would almost certainly be another
message from his Mum, checking that he
had actually left.

Glancing at the screen, though, Alfie
instantly realised it wasn't his Mum. Not
unless she had

a new number. And he was pretty sure
that, even if she had, it was unlikely to be
00000 000000.

Smiling to himself, Alfie clicked on the
message. He had a pretty good idea who
it would be from.

Tuesday

Chapter six

To say that Hayden Whitlock and
Reuben Ryan were surprised would be
an understatement. Flabbergasted better
summed it up.

Although neither teenager was a
stranger to receiving praise from
others regarding their various football
achievements, they had never expected
to receive a word of congratulations from
Jasper Johnson.

Yet at school on Tuesday morning, that's
exactly what happened.

"Wait for me you two," a voice had called
to them as they approached the school
gates.

Turning to see a red-faced Jasper
jogging determinedly in their direction,
Hayden and Reuben glanced quizzically

at one another. Surely he wasn't talking to them.

They were about to carry on walking, when they heard Jasper's voice again. "Hayden. Reuben. Wait there."

A confused expression remained etched on each boy's face as they waited for Jasper to catch them up. Neither boy could remember the last time Jasper had spoken to them. Yet here he was, seemingly desperate to chat. What could he want?

Moments later, Jasper was standing in front of the two friends. He was puffing and panting heavily. Desperately trying to get his breath back. He doubted whether he had ever jogged such a distance before school.

"I... just... wanted... to... say... well... done," he just about managed to gasp out loud, in-between deep, chugging breaths. "Brilliant... news... about... being... kept... on... at... United."

Hayden looked at Reuben and raised an eyebrow. Reuben merely shrugged his shoulders by way of response.

"Erm... Thanks Jasper," replied a clearly confused Hayden.

"No problem," Jasper continued, finally starting to overcome his breathlessness.

"It's a shame about Billy, though, isn't it? I felt really bad for him when I heard the news. He must be gutted?"

Hayden and Reuben both stared at Jasper, but said nothing. They didn't for one second believe that Jasper had been upset by Billy's failure to be kept on at Kingsway United. They were fully expecting the other boy to suddenly make an unpleasant comment. There was no way Jasper was being serious. Being kind just wasn't in his nature.

Realising that the other two boys were far from convinced by what he was saying, Jasper went into full-on acting mode.

"I really mean it," he exclaimed, trying his hardest to sound sincere. He wore a hurt expression on his face. "Look, I don't blame you for not believing me. I know I've been unkind in the past, but I'm not like that anymore. I'm older now. I've grown up. I've changed. Honestly!"

Jasper detested having to say these words. Even if he was only pretending. He simply hated having to be nice to people that he couldn't stand. Which was practically everyone.

Yet, if his plan was to succeed, he needed Reuben and Hayden to fully believe what he was saying.

The two friends continued to eye Jasper suspiciously. Unsure of what to make of what they were hearing. The other boy certainly seemed sincere. But this was Jasper Johnson. Hayden and Reuben knew only too well how devious he could be.

Sensing the two boys still weren't fully convinced by his display, Jasper started to worry. What could he possibly do to persuade the numpties that he really meant what he was saying? It took all of his self-control to avoid letting his frustration show.

Then he had an idea.

"I've been there, remember," he went on, sounding incredibly sad. "I know what it's like to be let go from an Academy. How it can feel to have your dreams snatched away from you. It's horrible. The worst feeling in the world." Now Jasper really did sound truly upset. Mainly because he was no longer acting. Recalling the memories of being released by the Kingsway United Academy still hurt dreadfully. More than he would ever admit.

The expressions on both Hayden and Reuben's faces instantly softened.

Suddenly Jasper's words seemed entirely genuine.

"Yeah. Billy was well gutted," Reuben finally answered. "We were both surprised that he was let go. I can't even imagine how shocked and disappointed he must have been."

"Well, if he ever wants to talk to someone who knows what he's going through, tell him he can always speak to me," Jasper said, attempting a caring tone. "I'd tell him myself, but I don't think he'd listen to me. Can you tell him that I've really changed? Please? And if he doesn't want to talk, please tell him that I'm really sorry that things didn't work out for him."

Just saying this final sentence left a sour taste in Jasper's mouth. He just hoped that they believed everything he was saying and would pass the message on.

Hayden and Reuben looked at each other again. Then Hayden nodded slightly. "We will Jasper. I promise."

"Thank you so much. I would really appreciate that," Jasper exclaimed joyfully. He couldn't help but think to himself that he deserved an award for this performance.

With that, he once more congratulated Hayden and Reuben for being kept on at the Academy, then said his goodbyes and made his way into school.

A wicked smirk appeared on his face the moment his back was turned towards the two boys.

His plan was underway.

***

Alfie could hardly believe his eyes. He rubbed them once. Then rubbed them again. The sight remained unchanged.

Hayden and Reuben were talking to Jasper!

Even though he was still a fair distance away, and the other boy had his back to him, Alfie knew immediately that it was Jasper. Hardly anybody else who attended Tideway Secondary School was as enormous as Jasper. Including most of the Year 11s. And a fair few of the teachers, come to that.

Although he desperately wanted to speak to Hayden and Reuben, he had absolutely no intention of talking to Jasper. None whatsoever. Instead he stopped by a bush where he could keep an eye on the trio whilst remaining out

of sight. He would catch up with his two
friends once Jasper had moved on.

As he waited, Alfie pulled his mobile
phone from the inside pocket of his school
blazer. For about the thousandth time, he
reread the message that he had received
the previous evening.

'Dreams do not always come true. But
this doesn't mean we should ever stop
dreaming! Always encourage your friends
to do the things they love. It's important
to never, ever let them give in. Your
future depends on it. MZ x'

It didn't take a genius to work out what
the message meant. Madam Zola was
clearly urging Alfie not to let Billy quit
playing football. Easy to say. Less easy
to do. Especially given his promise not
to mention the sport to his friend for the
foreseeable future.

It was the last part of the message that
concerned him the most. 'Your future
depends on it'. Did this mean that if
he couldn't get Billy playing football
again, then his own dream of becoming
a professional footballer wouldn't come
true? Alfie wasn't sure. To be safe,
though, he would do everything he
could to reignite his friend's passion for
football.

For the umpteenth time since receiving the message, he attempted to reply to it. For the umpteenth time, he received the same response.

'Number not recognised'

Feeling frustrated, Alfie peered around the bush to see whether his friends were still talking to Jasper. They were. What could they possibly be talking to him about? he wondered.

Replacing the mobile phone in his pocket, Alfie swung his bag off his shoulder, opened it, and took out a football. Back when he first started at Tideway, he used to bring a football with him for a lunchtime kickabout every day. He very rarely did now. Instead, he tended to spend most break and lunchtimes with Daisy.

Today, though, Alfie hoped to persuade his friends to join him in a lunchtime kick-about. Including Billy. While he had promised his best friend that he wouldn't waffle on about football for the time being, he had made no such guarantee that their other friends wouldn't.

Alfie was fairly certain that once Hayden, Reuben and some of the others heard that Billy was thinking about quitting football, they would be equally keen to talk him out of doing so. If one of them could persuade Billy to join in their lunchtime match, it would be a start.

Letting the ball fall to the floor, Alfie flicked it up with his left foot and began doing some keepy-uppies. He was just approaching the 50 mark, when he saw Jasper finally move away from Hayden and Reuben.

He snatched the ball out of the air, stuffed it back in his bag, and jogged in the direction of his friends.

He noticed that both Hayden and Reuben appeared to be somewhat baffled. "What did he want?" Alfie asked as he approached, not even bothering to say hello.

They quickly explained to Alfie about the conversation they'd just had with Jasper. As soon as they finished, Alfie snorted disbelievingly. "He's up to something," he declared confidently. "No doubt about it."

"I don't know, Alfie," Hayden replied. "He seemed different. Almost... human!"

Alfie snorted again. "Pah. The day Jasper Johnson becomes human is the day I become a mermaid."

This made his two friends laugh out loud. Once they had finished laughing,

Alfie told them about his trip to Billy's house. He explained how low spirited their friend had seemed. How he'd claimed that he didn't want anything to do with football anymore. He declined to mention that he had come away from the visit with a copy of the latest FIFA game. He figured this may make it look like he was taking advantage of the situation. Anyway, he'd give the game back to Billy once his friend was interested in football again. Probably.

He also didn't say anything about the message from Madam Zola. None of his friends knew about the fortune teller. She had once warned him to keep it that way.

Both Hayden and Reuben agreed that they should encourage Billy not to give up playing football. They were also quite excited by the prospect of having a lunchtime kick about. The football season had ended some weeks ago and both boys were desperate for a bit of footy action.

Reuben promised to get Liam Walker and, maybe, Chloe Reed to join in the game. He had maths with them both first thing and would ask them then. Hayden said that he would ask Billy, although stressed that he wouldn't pressure him into playing. Not yet. It was too soon.

Alfie agreed and said he would ask a few other children to play as well.

Arranging to meet outside the gym at break time, the three boys wandered into the school grounds and went their separate ways.

Alfie was supposed to be meeting Daisy in the common room before registration. Glancing at his watch, and realising he was a bit late, he was just about to pick up his pace, when he caught sight of Jasper. He was standing at the opposite end of the corridor. Seemingly looking directly at him. Then, in a flash, he was gone.

Seeing Jasper made Alfie think about what Hayden and Reuben had just told him. He refused to believe that Jasper was really upset by Billy's failure to be retained by Kingsway United. Or that he was truly happy for Hayden and Reuben.

Jasper was up to something. There was little doubt about that. The key question, though, was what?

Chapter seven

By morning break, the lunchtime match was starting to take shape.

Practically all of those who had been asked to join in the game had said yes. Only Billy had said no.

"He wasn't interested at all," Hayden told Alfie as they, and a small group of Year 8s, sat on a picnic bench located outside the school gym. "He got quite cross when I asked him. Wanted to know if it was your idea."

Alfie's heart skipped a beat. He didn't want Billy to think he was already breaking the promise he'd made to him. Not after less than a day. "What did you say?"

Hayden chuckled as he detected the concern in his friend's voice. "Don't worry.

I told him it was my idea. Not sure that he believed me, mind you."

"That's probably because you've never had an idea before, H," Chloe Reed giggled. Chloe was one of Alfie's oldest friends. She had been a former teammate of his at the Kingsway Colts until she left to join a girls' team. Chloe was one of the best footballers Alfie knew. She was also responsible for introducing him to Daisy.

"Anyway, we've got enough players for five-a-side," Hayden continued, ignoring Chloe's jape. "Should be good fun."

Alfie was disappointed, if not overly surprised, at Billy's refusal to play. He knew it had been a long-shot but figured it was worth a try.

"Did you say anything to him about our chat with Jasper?" Reuben asked.

Hayden nodded. "Yeah. I think it's fair to say that he won't be talking his feelings through with him anytime soon."

"So he wasn't interested in Jasper's 'kind' offer then?" Alfie inquired in a heavily sarcastic tone.

"You could say that," Hayden answered. "I think he trusts Jasper about as much as you do."

"I still think he was just trying to be nice," Reuben mused. "He didn't seem to have any intention of being nasty."

"You don't know him as well as we do," Alfie countered. "He's always up to something."

"I'm not sure, Alfie," Hayden said. "You didn't see him this morning. I've never seen him like that before. I really thought he was going to cry when he was talking about what it was like to be let go by the United Academy. I think he may have been telling the truth, as well."

"Wow, H. You've been thinking? That must have given you a headache," Chloe joked. Everyone burst out laughing. Well, everyone apart from Hayden.

"Ha ha, Chloe. Very funny. You really should think about becoming a comedian," he moaned.

As the end of break time neared, the group's conversation turned towards what the teams for the match should be.

"If we pick sides now, it will save time at lunch," Liam Walker suggested. "That'll give us longer game time."

Liam was another of Alfie's former Colts' teammates. He was a natural goalscorer and had finished top scorer for the team in every season that he had played for them.

Liam was one of the only original

members of the Kingsway Colts who still played for the team.

The gang agreed that Liam's idea was a good one and set about the task of picking fair teams. It would have been easier to wrestle a lion with your hands tied together. Try as they might, the friends just could not agree on what was fair and what wasn't. No matter what was suggested, there was always someone who would grumble, "these teams aren't fair."

At one point, Alfie had moaned that Hayden and Reuben shouldn't be allowed to be on the same team as they both played for an Academy. It was only when Liam pointed out that he played for an Academy himself that Alfie had begrudgingly accepted the decision to let them be on the same team. Matty and Noel were right. He really did need to have more confidence in his own ability!

Eventually, after a good few minutes of squabbling, the teams were finally agreed upon. Not everyone was happy, but that was tough luck. Those who were moaning would either have to get on with it or go and do something else at lunchtime instead. It was simply impossible to please everyone.

Moments later, the bell sounded to signal the end of break. The friends stood up and agreed to meet out on the field at lunch time as promptly as possible. It would be up to whoever got to the field first to secure an area where they could set up a pitch.

Sitting in his English lesson a little later on, Alfie was finding it almost impossible to concentrate on the chapter of the book he was supposed to be reading. Aside from football magazines, he didn't really enjoy reading that much. It just didn't interest him. Today, though, he was finding it even harder than usual to focus on the words in front of him. As he struggled through the third chapter of Lord of the Flies, all he could think about was Billy.

He was desperate for his friend to see them playing the lunchtime match. Alfie was sure that if he did, then he would be overcome by the desire to join in.

He recalled being in a similar situation a few years earlier. Back when he attended Kingsway Junior School. On that occasion, Alfie was sulking and had declined to take part in a break-time match. The Kingsway Colts were bottom of the league and most of his friends seemed to be thinking about leaving the team. He had felt angry and betrayed. However, watching his friends playing football, while he sat miserably by himself at the side of the playground, was agonising. By lunchtime he had swallowed his pride and was back playing.

He just hoped that Billy would feel the exact same way.

Chapter eight

At the very moment that Alfie was sat worrying about Billy, over in the science block Hayden was having a conversation with Jasper for the second time that day.

The two boys had been in the same science class for the best part of two years. During this time, they had largely ignored each other. Yet today they were actually sitting side-by-side, working together.

"Hayden, over here. I've saved you a seat," Jasper had called out as Hayden wandered into the classroom after break. He said it in a way that made it sound as though the two boys had been long-term best buddies.

Judging by the expression on Hayden's face, you could have been forgiven for thinking that someone had just asked him to explain quantum physics in five words or less. He could not think of one single reason why Jasper would want to sit next to him. Or, more importantly, why he would want to sit next to Jasper.

Noticing that his usual seat was already occupied by the boy who normally sat next to Jasper, and unable to see a space anywhere else, Hayden had no choice but to reluctantly accept the offer.

For the opening half-hour of the lesson, neither boy said a word to each other. They just sat there in silence, listening, or at least pretending to listen, to the class teacher waffle on about the periodic table.

However, when Mrs Bertram asked the children to work with the person sitting next to them to conduct a simple experiment, the two were forced to converse with each other.

Yet rather than discussing the boiling and melting points of certain elements, like they were supposed to be, Jasper had a different topic of conversation in mind.

"I don't suppose you've had a chance to talk to Billy yet?" he whispered, as Hayden began setting up a Bunsen burner.

Hayden was just about to bluntly tell him that Billy wasn't the slightest bit interested in his offer, when he suddenly paused. He was surprised to find that he didn't want to hurt Jasper's feelings. Ever since their chat earlier that morning, Hayden had started to feel slightly more sympathetic towards Jasper. Maybe he really was starting to change. They were getting older, after all.

Instead, Hayden replied, "Erm. No, not yet. I'll try to speak to him this afternoon." He figured this would give him more time to think of a way to break Billy's response to Jasper in a more delicate manner.

The larger boy faked a look of disappointment. "That's a shame," he sighed despondently. "I'd really like to help him."

Once again, Hayden felt a pang of sympathy for Jasper. He really did seem to be trying hard to do the right thing.

For a few minutes, the boys concentrated on the set task. They took turns to carefully hold an element over the Bunsen burners' flame, while the other recorded what happened. They worked surprisingly well together. A fact that Hayden remarked upon.

Realising that Hayden was starting to trust him, Jasper smiled slyly to himself. It was time to put the next part of his plan into action.

"How's Alfie getting on at Norton Town?" he asked quietly, as Hayden busied himself with writing something in his workbook. "Has he heard whether he's being kept on next season?"

Jasper knew full well that Alfie had been retained by Norton. He'd heard enough people talking about it over the past couple of days. Yet he wanted Hayden to believe that he knew nothing about it. He needed the other boy to believe his reaction.

Instantly, Hayden began to eye Jasper suspiciously. He carefully searched the other boy's face for any signs that he was about to be unkind. It was no secret that Jasper absolutely despised Alfie. More than he did anyone else.

Yet there was no trace of unkindness on Jasper's face. He looked almost angelic. This alone should have set alarm bells ringing. It should have been enough to warn Hayden that something wasn't quite right. It didn't. Jasper's acting had successfully convinced Hayden to trust him.

Deciding that the other boy was asking out of interest rather than malice, Hayden eventually explained to Jasper that Alfie had indeed been kept on at the Norton Town Academy for another season.

"Oh!" Jasper exclaimed, a little louder than he had meant to. He sounded genuinely shocked. "Well that's... erm... that's brilliant," he stuttered, bringing the volume of his voice back down to barely more than a whisper.

Hayden smiled. "You're gutted, aren't you? It's no secret that you hate Alfie," he replied, careful to also keep his voice as quiet as possible.

Jasper lent back in his stool, as though Hayden had struck him. A horrified expression appeared on his face. He knew he was slightly overacting, but he couldn't help himself. He was really starting to enjoy this. "I wouldn't say I hate him. Okay, I admit I used to. But, as I said earlier, I'm older now. I've changed."

"So why did you seem so disappointed when I told you that he'd been kept on by Norton?" Hayden inquired.

"I wasn't disappointed," Jasper protested. He paused for a moment, as if carefully considering his next words. "I was just... a bit surprised."

Noticing Mrs Bertram glaring angrily in their direction, the two boys stopped talking for a moment and diligently got on with conducting another experiment. Once they were convinced that their teacher was no longer paying them any attention, they resumed their conversation, speaking even quieter than they previously had been.

"Why are you surprised?" Hayden hissed. "Alfie's a really good player."

Hearing this proved to be a real test of Jasper's acting ability. He wanted to scowl at Hayden. Tell the other boy that Alfie wasn't a good player at all. That he was rubbish and had just got really lucky. Instead, he raised his hands innocently and whispered "I didn't mean that. I know he's a really good player." He almost had to force the words out. "It's just that... look, if you had asked me back when I played for the Kingsway Colts who I thought had more chance of making it as a professional footballer, Alfie or Billy, then I would have said Billy. He was amazing. Easily the best player on the team. At least until you came along. You can't honestly tell me that if someone had asked you the same question, you wouldn't have said the same?"

Before Hayden could answer, Jasper quickly stood up and thrust his right hand into one of his trouser pockets. "Sorry, just need to get my spare pen," he explained. "Mine has just run out." A second or two later, his hand reappeared holding a blue biro. He waved it deliberately in the air, then sat back on his stool and looked directly at the other boy. "Honestly, hand on heart, who would you say is the better player. Billy or Alfie?"

Hayden considered the question carefully. Then slowly nodded his head. "I suppose Billy is a bit better. I mean Alfie is still really good, but when he's on form Billy can be class. Some of his skills are ridiculously good!"

Jasper smiled. The response was perfect.

"So, you agree that it's a bit of a surprise that Alfie is in an Academy when Billy isn't," he continued, maintaining his innocent tone.

"Yeah, I guess so. But..." Before Hayden could say anything further, Mrs Bertram's voice halted the conversation.

"Okay everybody. You should all be pretty much done by now. So finish off what you're doing. We've got 15 minutes until lunchtime and I want everything put away safely and tidily before you go to lunch. Leave your workbooks on the desk so that I can check what you've done."

Once the teacher had finished giving her instructions, Hayden turned to continue what he had been about to say to Jasper. However, the seat next to him was empty. Jasper was already over the other side of the classroom, putting the Bunsen burner and some test tubes away.

Knowing that Hayden could only see the back of his head, Jasper allowed an evil smirk to spread right across his face.

He gently patted the pocket he had taken the pen from a few minutes earlier. It would be fair to say that his conversation with Hayden could not have gone any better.

Chapter nine

The lunchtime match was in full swing. Any fears the children had about the teams being unfair had proved totally unfounded.

The game had swung to-and-fro. The lead changing hands on numerous occasions.

There were now ten minutes' left until the end of lunch. Alfie's team were winning 11-9. This was largely down to Alfie's own performance. Sure, Liam had scored eight of the team's goals, but Alfie had played sensationally.

Although it was only a friendly kick-around, Alfie was determined to display a more confident side to his game. He was demanding the ball from his teammates at every opportunity. Trying to pass forward as often as possible – especially when his team were attacking. He'd even attempted and, on a couple of occasions, actually succeeded, in outskilling both Hayden and Reuben.

There had still been the odd moment where Alfie found himself gawping in awe as Hayden and Reuben performed impossible looking tricks. However, instead of merely believing that such skills were beyond him, today he had decided to attempt some of them himself. To his surprise, after a couple of tries, he realised that he was able to do most of them just as competently as his friends could.

The one frustration Alfie had was that Billy had not yet wandered onto the field. He had kept half-an-eye out for his best friend since the start of lunch. Yet Billy was nowhere to be seen. He quickly removed his phone from his pocket and checked the time. 12:50. Ten minutes until the end of lunch. He seriously doubted his plan to tempt Billy into a game of football was going to be successful. Not today, at least.

Turning his attention back to the match, Alfie watched as Liam sent a shot inches the wrong side of a black rucksack which was being used as a goalpost. Then he heard Chloe shout the words he'd been dreading hearing. "Alfie, it's your turn in goal." He hated going in goal. Absolutely despised it. Mainly because he was not a very good goalkeeper. In fact, he was awful.

Not for the first time that lunch time, he pretended not to hear the call. Hopeful that, if he hesitated, one of his teammates would volunteer to have another turn in goal. They didn't. This time there was no getting out of it.

"Do I have to?" he moaned.

"Yes," Chloe answered. "Everyone else has been in for ten minutes. Now it's your turn for until the end of lunch. It's only fair."

Head bowed, he moped sulkily over to the makeshift goal. "I'm not diving for any balls," he whinged under his breath. "Not getting my uniform dirty." Every player involved in the game smiled. They all knew Alfie detested going in goal.

To make a bad situation even worse, upon reaching the goal and raising his head, he noticed that Daisy was now standing at the side of the pitch, talking to some of her friends. Minutes earlier, when he'd been playing so well, he would not have minded one bit if his girlfriend was watching the game. Yet she wasn't around. Now that it was time for him to go in goal, she had suddenly appeared. Typical!

It wasn't long before the reluctant goalkeeper was called into action. A long pass from Hayden was controlled expertly by Reuben on his chest. He easily took the ball around the last defender and within seconds was bearing down on Alfie's goal.

Deciding that his best option would be to try and tackle Reuben rather than attempt to save his shot, Alfie raced off his line. His opponent, though, had guessed that this was what Alfie would do. As Alfie approached him, Reuben wrapped his kicking leg around the back of his standing leg and struck the ball hard. Reuben loved performing this trick; the 'rabona'. He spent hours practicing and was something of an expert at it.

Alfie had not been prepared for the trick. He watched helplessly as the perfectly struck ball raced past him and into the goal. "Get in there," Reuben yelled. He playfully ruffled the embarrassed goalkeeper's curly blonde hair. Despite himself, Alfie couldn't help

but raise a rueful smile. Sometimes you just had to hold your hands up and admit that you'd been outdone by a brilliant piece of skill. This was one of those times.

Moments later the game was level. At the urging of his teammates, a boy called Charlie shot from long distance. The strike wasn't particularly powerful, but it was on target. And, given Alfie's lack of goalkeeping ability, that was enough. As the ball crept goalward, Alfie half-heartedly bent down to reach the ball. He got nowhere near it. The ball rolled slowly past Alfie's barely extended arm and crossed between the two school bags which marked the goal.

"Alfie," Liam whined from the other end of the pitch. "You could at least try to save it."

"I did tell you I wasn't going to dive," Alfie replied miserably.

Within two minutes the turnaround was complete; albeit in slightly controversial circumstances. This time there was little Alfie could do to stop the goal. Hayden wriggled past two challenges and arrowed a shot towards the far post. Well... bag. No 'keeper would have got anywhere near it.

However, the ball skimmed the side of the bag. "No goal..." Alfie called instantly. "... hit the post."

"No way," Hayden argued. "That would have easily gone in off the post in a real goal."

"Nah. Would have definitely bounced out," Liam claimed, backing up Alfie's argument.

After a good 30 seconds or so of debate, Alfie and Liam begrudgingly accepted that it was a goal. They had to really. Their other three teammates all agreed with Hayden's argument that the ball would definitely have bounced off the post and into the goal.

Alfie had been in goal for less than

five minutes. In that time, his team had gone from leading the match 11-9, to trailing 12-11. He looked over towards Daisy, desperately hoping that she was still talking to her friends. He didn't want her to have seen any of his hopeless goalkeeping performance. He was out of luck. His girlfriend smiled sympathetically at him and held her arms out wide, as if offering to give him a cuddle. This only served to irritate him even further.

Thankfully, his goalkeeping ordeal stopped there. Fed up with his sulking, not to mention his inability to save anything, Chloe offered to go back in goal. It was an offer Alfie gleefully accepted. He quickly jogged away from the goal, as if by just being near it he could somehow be sucked back into his least favourite position.

"How much longer have we got left?" Reuben asked no one in particular.

Alfie glanced at his phone. "Just under five minutes," he replied.

"Let's get on with it then," Liam shouted. "We need to get a goal back." From the serious tone in his voice, you could have been forgiven for thinking the World Cup was on the line.

Restarting the game from a goal-kick, Chloe passed the ball out to Alfie, who had found space on the left-hand side of the pitch. It was a routine pass and should have been easy for a player of Alfie's ability to control. But as the ball rolled smoothly towards him, something to the side of the pitch caught his attention. Instead of trapping the ball, like he should have done, it went straight under his foot and out for a throw-in.

"Concentrate Alfie," Liam grumbled. He hated losing. Even a meaningless lunchtime kick-around like this.

At that particular moment, though, there was only one thing that Alfie was paying attention to. The person who was plodding slowly in the direction of the pitch. Billy.

Alfie watched as his best friend wandered towards the playing area. He held up his hand and waved to his friend. Billy responded with the same gesture, but stopped walking just before he reached them.

This was exactly what Alfie had been waiting for. The chance to entice Billy into the game. He realised he needed to do something to impress his friend. Something amazing that would remind

Billy just what a great game football could be, and he needed to do it quickly. The lunch hour was nearly over.

Refocussing on the game, Alfie went in search of the ball. Annoyingly, he could see that Hayden and Reuben were currently indulging in a spot of keep-ball. They had Alfie's teammates chasing shadows. Just as it seemed one of them was about to lose possession of the ball, he would produce a sublime piece of skill to get himself out of trouble, then nudge the ball on to his equally talented teammate.

"Watch the ball, not their feet," Alfie called to his teammates, as he ran over to assist them. Liam took the advice on board. Rather than just diving into a challenge he jockeyed his opponent, trying to force him into making a mistake. Once or twice Reuben tried to tempt Liam into a challenge. "Just stand him up," Alfie called. "Don't let him fool you."

With nowhere to go, Reuben decided to try and confuse his friend by attempting a rabona pass to Hayden. Liam, though, was not to be fooled. He managed to just about get a toe onto the ball as it left Reuben's foot. It was only an ever-soslight touch, but it was enough to divert the ball away from its intended target.

Hayden and Alfie both sprinted after the loose ball. They reached it at the exact same time, causing the ball to ricochet up into the air. Alfie reacted first. Without letting it bounce, he used his right foot to scoop the ball over his head. Quick as a flash, he spun on his heel and cushioned the ball with his right knee. Then, shifting his weight so that his right foot was planted firmly on the grass, he volleyed the ball with his left foot. He caught it perfectly. The ball flew through the air. It was struck with so much force that, even though it was aimed straight at the opposition goalkeeper, there was no way he was going to attempt to save it. In fact, he more or less dived out of the way.

"What a goal," Liam yelled.

Everyone, from both teams, stood and applauded. It was a truly outstanding goal. A beaming smile lit up Alfie's face.

Turning to see what affect his wonder goal had had on his friend, the smile instantly turned to a frown. Billy was no longer watching. Instead he was striding back in the direction of the school. Moments later he entered the school building and was out of sight. He hadn't turned around to face the pitch once.

From the side of the pitch, Alfie heard Daisy holler her approval. He barely registered the fact that his girlfriend had finally seen him do something good.

He merely felt frustrated. His plan had failed.

Chapter ten

At the opposite end of the field, sitting on a bench located a safe distance away from the pitch, Jasper had been watching. Waiting.

For a moment, he had been worried. For a moment, he thought that Billy was going to give in to temptation. That he was going to join in the match.

He had taken a step towards the pitch. One more step and he would have been on it. No doubt asking someone if he could join in.

But then he had seemingly changed his mind. Rather than walk onto the pitch, he had instead spun around and walked away.

He hadn't even stayed long enough to

see that little muppet score his flukey goal.

Jasper breathed a huge sigh of relief. Had Billy joined in the game, all his careful planning could have been ruined. He needed Billy to remain fed up with football for as long as possible.

Realising there were only a few minutes' left before the bell rang to signal the end of lunch, Jasper briefly contemplated delaying the next stage of his plan. He was unsure whether he had enough time to do what needed to be done. The thought of finally getting one over on Alfie ultimately convinced him to press ahead. There should be just about enough time. So long as he was quick.

He waited for Billy to enter the school building, then stood up and hurried after his prey.

Seconds later he was through the door. There were children everywhere! All of them wearing identical blazers. He craned his neck, desperately searching the busy corridor for Billy. Eventually he located him leaning against a wall outside a classroom. He was alone. Perfect.

Jasper took his mobile phone out of his trouser pocket and checked the time.

12:58. Roughly two minutes until the bell was due to sound. Long enough.

Quickly, Jasper stalked towards Billy. As he did so, he was careful not to look directly at him. He didn't want the other boy to think that this was a planned meeting. Not that Billy would have noticed. He was paying absolutely no attention to anything going on around him. He was just staring up at the ceiling, completely lost in his own thoughts.

At first, Jasper took a step past Billy, trying to make it seem as though he hadn't seen him. Then, as if noticing him for the first time, he swung his bulky frame around so that he was standing face-to-face with the other boy.

"Oh, hi Billy," Jasper said in a friendly tone. "I was hoping I'd bump into you sooner or later."

Billy didn't reply. Just carried on staring miserably up at the ceiling.

"Look, I know you don't like me," he continued, ignoring the fact that he was himself being ignored. "But I just wanted to tell you that I know what it's like to be let go from the Academy. How gutting it can be. I was devastated when it happened to me." Jasper's voice quavered with emotion as he once again recalled the memory of rejection. "If you ever need someone to talk to, I'm here for you."

Slowly, Billy lowered his eyes until he was looking directly at Jasper's face. The other boy was so much taller than he was that he didn't have to lower them too far. "I know. Hayden has already told me," he replied disinterestedly. "I don't want to speak to anyone about it. Least of all you!" With that, he resumed staring at the ceiling.

This news surprised Jasper. Hayden had told him that he hadn't spoken to Billy yet. Why had he lied? No matter. It wasn't important. In fact, it may even work to his advantage. It might make his offer sound even more convincing.

Hoping that he hadn't let his surprise show, Jasper bowed his head, as though disappointed by Billy's response. "Fair enough," he said, raising his hands in a defeated manner. "If you change your mind, I'm sure you'll be able to find me." He made as if to walk off, then suddenly stopped. "Still, I suppose it must be harder for you, in a way."

Billy rolled his eyes. Without thinking, he asked "Why must it?"

"Well, when I was let go I didn't

have any other friends who were in an Academy. You've got Hayden and Reuben." Then, after a short pause, he added, as if he'd only just thought of it, "And Alfie, of course. I forgot about him. He's at Norton Town, isn't he? That must be really hard for you. I mean, I know Alfie has got better... but he's nowhere near as good as you."

Billy shook his head sadly. "Is this supposed to be making me feel better? Because it isn't."

"I'm sorry," Jasper continued, hoping he sounded sincere. "It's just weird to think of Alfie being in an Academy when you're not. You were always the best player for the Colts back when I played."

He paused again and quickly glanced at Billy. He could see that the other boy was now frowning.

A seed of doubt had been planted in his mind.

"I was talking to Hayden before lunch," Jasper continued. "He's really surprised, too. He told me that he thinks you're a much better player than Alfie."

The somewhat one-sided conversation was suddenly interrupted by the clanging of the school bell.

"Well, I've got to get to my next class

now," Jasper said, once the ringing had stopped. "But like I said, if you ever want to talk…" He left the offer hanging, then strolled off. Leaving Billy alone with his thoughts.

Upon reaching the other end of the corridor, Jasper turned around and glanced towards Billy. He could see that the other boy was still staring at the ceiling. But the expression on his face had undoubtedly changed. It was a mixture of thoughtfulness, confusion and anger.

Jasper crossed his fingers. Hopefully Billy would be thinking carefully about what he had just said.

Chapter eleven

Alfie was sitting in his room playing FIFA
when he heard it. He was so absorbed in
the game that for a moment he ignored
the sound and continued playing. Then
he realised what it was.

T-ting-a-ching. T-ting-a-ching. T-ting-a-ching.

Pausing the game, Alfie tossed the Xbox
controller onto his bed, then dived across
the mattress, snatching the phone off his
bedside table.

"Hello," he answered excitably. He didn't
even bother to look at the screen. There
was no need to. He knew it wouldn't
display who was calling. And anyway, he
already knew who it was.

There was only one person whose
calls were announced by a wind chime

ringtone. Madam Zola.

There was a short blast of static. It was so loud that Alfie momentarily had to hold the phone away from his ear. Then there was silence. For a while, Alfie thought that the person on the other end had hung up. Then, very faintly, he heard a muffled voice.

"Hello. Alfie? Alfie? Alfie? Can you hear me? It's Madam Zola."

The voice was so hushed that he had to strain his ears to make out what the elderly fortune teller was saying.

"Just about," he replied, raising the volume of his voice to slightly above its normal level. "Can you hear me?"

There was no immediate reply. Then, very softly, he heard Madam Zola again.

"Hello, Alfie. Are you there? I can't hear you. I think your phone is playing up."

Puzzled, Alfie removed the phone from his ear and looked at the screen.

As expected, he had full signal. He'd never had a problem like this before in his bedroom. It must be her phone that was faulty.

He pressed the phone tight against the side of his face and spoke louder than before. "Yes. I'm here. My phone is fine. Can you call me back? Where are you?"

"Ohhh, I think I heard something that time," Madam Zola replied. Alfie could still barely hear what she was saying. "No idea what you said, though. Sounds like you're mumbling. You really should think about getting a new phone. The one you've got is obviously broken."

Alfie rolled his eyes. His phone was fine. He'd been speaking to Daisy on it only ten minutes earlier. "It's really hard to hear you." He was practically shouting now. "Can you talk a bit louder?"

"Walk split powder?" Madam Zola repeated, totally mishearing. "What are you talking about Alfie? You are a very strange boy at times. Look, I'll just assume you can hear me even if I can't hear you. I haven't got time for all these silly shenanigans. I'm a very busy woman."

The teenager could still barely hear what the fortune teller was saying. However, as trying to get her to speak up was proving to be an utter waste of time, he instead concentrated his energies on listening to what she had to say.

"Now..." the fortune teller continued. Her voice still sounded no louder than a whisper. "... I know you're trying your best to encourage Billy to play football again. Well done for that. Keep trying, but don't push too hard. The most important thing right now is that you're there for him. It's when we're feeling down that we need our friends the most. However, it's also when we're feeling upset that we're most likely to say and do things that we don't really mean."

"Like what?" Alfie shouted.

"Bike shop?" Madam Zola exclaimed. "What are you banging on about? Anyway, just be quiet and let me finish saying what I've got to say. There are certain people who just love stirring trou..."

Without warning, the faint sound of Madam Zola's voice faded completely. There was a moment of absolute silence. Then the quiet was replaced by another deafening crackle of static. Yet again, Alfie was forced to hold the phone away from his ear. When he could no longer hear the crackling, he brought it back beside his ear. Seconds later Madam Zola's muffled voice returned. It was even quieter than before. "Do you understand what I'm saying, Alfie?"

"No," Alfie screamed down the phone. "Your voice disappeared. I didn't hear you. Can you repeat what you said?

"Can I complete hot stew bread? You've gone mad, Alfie. Stark raving bonkers. Anyway, I really must be going now. Speak soon. Bye."

"No, don't go," he yelled at the top of his voice. "Please don't go. No. No Noooooo!"

But there was no reply. Madam Zola had ended the call.

Irritated, Alfie flung himself back on his bed and let out a howl of pure frustration.

Within seconds, his bedroom door flew open. His younger sister, Megan, entered the room. There was an expression of mock concern on her face.

"Oh dear, have you just had an argument with Daisy?" she teased.

"No," Alfie snapped. "Go away Megan. I'm not in the mood."

"Then why else would you be shouting 'don't go' at the top of your voice? I don't think I've ever heard you two have an argument before," Megan continued. She loved winding her brother up. "It's okay. I'm sure you'll make it up with her."

"It's got nothing to do with Daisy, okay. It wasn't even her on the phone."

Before he had a chance to move, Megan swooped towards her brother's bedside table and grabbed his phone. Alfie rolled off the bed to confront her. He was too slow. Megan had already brought up the list of his recent phone calls. The last call Alfie had received was from Daisy 15 minutes earlier.

"Ha. I knew it." Megan laughed triumphantly.

"Get out of my room Moggy," Alfie shouted angrily. He snatched the phone from his sister's hand. Then, perhaps more roughly than he should have done, forcibly marched his sibling out of his bedroom and slammed the door shut behind her.

No doubt Megan would go straight to their parents. She'd be moaning that Alfie had hurt her when he had pushed her out of his room. He would probably find himself in big trouble in a few minutes' time. But right now he couldn't care less.

The only thing on his mind was the call he had just had from Madam Zola. She had been trying to warn him about something. He was sure that before her voice had momentarily disappeared she had said something about someone wanting to stir trouble.

Immediately, Alfie's thoughts turned to Jasper. Lying on his bed, he recalled what Hayden and Reuben had told him earlier that day about his nemesis seemingly having changed. He hadn't believed it for one moment when they'd said it then.

He certainly didn't believe it now.

Wednesday

Chapter twelve

Chloe Reed glanced angrily at her watch.

She had agreed to meet Reuben Ryan outside the newsagents at eight o'clock sharp. It was now two minutes to. He was still nowhere to be seen.

She took a deep breath as she battled to control her anger. Did Reuben not realise that when a girl arranged to meet you somewhere at a certain time, then you were supposed to turn up early? Arriving late to a first date, or even on time, was hardly a promising start to a new relationship!

In fairness to Reuben, he might have aimed to be more punctual had he realised that he was supposed to be going on a date. When Chloe had asked him if he wanted to walk to school with her, he had assumed that it was just two friends arranging to meet up before school. Nothing more, nothing less. He had no idea that this early morning meeting was being classed as a 'date'.

Yet this was exactly how Chloe viewed it. She had liked Reuben for ages and had tried to ask him out numerous times before. Whenever she tried, though, someone else, usually Hayden, was always around. Spoiling her plans. The two boys had become inseparable over the past year. It was extremely rare to see one without the other. However, Chloe knew that Hayden had a dentist appointment this morning and would be going into school late. This was her perfect chance to finally get Reuben alone.

And now he was late! Or two minutes away from being late. Which, in Chloe's mind, was much the same thing.

Peeking at her watch again, and realising that a whole minute had passed since she had last checked, the girl was just about to stomp off when she heard footsteps coming from behind her.

"Where have you been?" she asked irritatedly, swivelling to face her late...

well, on-time... 'date'. "You're late!"

Turning to face Reuben, Chloe's heart sank to the pit of her stomach. He wasn't alone. She could have screamed.

Why was he walking with him of all people?

"What's he doing here?" Chloe demanded, gesturing dismissively at the unwanted companion.

"Erm... I just met him on the way here. I'm not late, am I?" Reuben inquired, sounding a tad confused. He grabbed his phone out of his pocket and checked the time. "I thought we agreed to meet at eight o'clock?"

"We did," Chloe agreed.

"But my phone says it's eight o'clock exactly," Reuben responded. "I'm on time."

"Yes." Chloe continued, unable to hide the frustration from her voice. "But you were supposed to be early."

"Oh? Why?" Reuben answered. The tone of total confusion was matched by the expression on his face.

"You just were!" Chloe took a deep breath, trying not to let the anger that was boiling up inside her show. "Anyway, we should get going. We don't want to be late for school. Say goodbye to... him...

and let's go."

"Chloe, there's no need to be rude,"
Reuben scolded. "We're in the middle of a
conversation. Anyway, I said he can walk
to school with us. That's alright, isn't it?"

Chloe looked at Jasper Johnson.
She didn't even try to keep the scowl
of displeasure from her face. Jasper
returned the look with his best attempt
at an innocent expression. It was a look
intended to say, 'I didn't ask to walk to

school with you, but, hey, what can I do?'

No, Chloe wanted to scream at the top her voice. No, he can't walk to school with us. It's just supposed to be us walking to school. Me and you. Together! Plus, I don't even like him. Not even a little bit. He's a scheming, manipulative, horrible bully!

Instead she merely shrugged her shoulders. "Whatever," she moaned, letting out an exasperated sigh. Without waiting for the other two, she spun on her heels and began marching purposely towards school. Reuben and Jasper had to half jog to catch her up. Once they had, the three teenagers spent the next five minutes advancing towards school in an awkward silence.

Eventually, Jasper was the first to speak. "Look, if I'm not wanted here, then I can always leave you two alone," he offered, in what he hoped was a sincere tone.

Chloe was just about to gleefully wave goodbye to the unwanted presence but before she could, Reuben answered. "Don't be silly. Stay, Jasper. Chloe, I know you don't like Jasper that much, but I happened to bump into him on my way to meet you this morning. We were talking about how upset Billy is at the moment and trying to come up with ideas of how we can make him feel better."

"And why would he..." Chloe nodded her head scornfully in Jasper's direction, "... care about making Billy feel better? He doesn't even like Billy. He doesn't like anyone."

"Look," said Jasper, sounding more than a little hurt by Chloe's words. "I really don't want to get in the way here. I'm obviously upsetting Chloe and I really don't mean to be." 'Although it is a bonus,' he thought silently to himself, while at the same time battling to keep the smirk from his face. "I was just offering my help as I'm the only other person around here who knows exactly how it feels to be let go by the United Academy," he continued. "Billy won't speak to me. I've already tried. But he will speak to you. Anyway, I should go."

Jasper bowed his head sadly and despondently started to plod across the road. He really was starting to master the art of acting. Maybe a career in Hollywood beckoned?

Reuben shot Chloe a look designed to make her feel guilty. Although she didn't feel in the slightest bit bad about Jasper supposedly being sad, she simply couldn't bare Reuben looking at her like that.

"Fine," she sighed. "You can walk with us," she called across the road to Jasper. She stopped short of saying please to the gigantic boy, though. She certainly didn't say sorry. She would never, ever apologise to Jasper. Not for anything.

"Are you sure you don't mind?" he replied, still sounding hurt. He was really beginning to enjoy himself now.

Chloe looked at Reuben again. The same expression was still plastered on his face. "I'm sure," she said, with all the enthusiasm she could muster. Which wasn't much.

Jasper paused, as if weighing up his options, then crossed back over the road towards the other two. He allowed himself a quick, sly grin as he did so. The morning was working out even better than he had intended. While he had fully planned to bump into Reuben on the way to school, he had no idea that the other boy was due to be meeting Chloe. That was just an added bonus. Yet the next few minutes would determine exactly how successful the morning's venture would be.

"So, Jasper," Reuben said, once the

larger boy had rejoined them. "Just before we met with Chloe you were telling me about your talk with Billy yesterday."

"Oh, yes. That's right," Jasper replied, as if he had only just recalled what they had been talking about. In reality, he had been waiting for the conversation to return to this point.

"Yeah, it didn't go well," Jasper sighed, giving a rueful shake of his head. "In fact, if anything I probably ended up making him feel sadder than he felt before."

"Surprise, surprise," Chloe muttered sarcastically under her breath. Another hard stare from Reuben stopped her from saying anything further.

"Anyway," Jasper continued, shrugging off Chloe's interruption. "I reckon he must have a chance of getting in at another team, don't you? He's a class player, after all."

"Definitely," Reuben agreed.

"Without a doubt," Chloe confirmed. "When I played for the Colts Billy was much better than anyone else in the team. At least until Hayden started playing. They were both as good as each other. He'll definitely get a trial with someone else."

Jasper could not have hoped for a better

response.

Realising this was his perfect opportunity, he slipped his hands into his trouser pockets and looked purposefully at Chloe. He felt like a snake that had just cornered a mouse. He just hoped he didn't look like one, too.

"Would you say he was a much better player than Alfie then?" Jasper asked, trying his absolute best to make it sound like it was an innocent question.

"Well…" Chloe considered the question carefully. "… maybe Billy's just a little bit better," she answered after a short pause. "Back then he was much better. But Alfie's really improved. There's not much between them anymore."

"He could do with being a bit more confident, though," Reuben added. "Sometimes when he plays for the school team he looks a bit nervous. If he believed in himself a bit more then he could probably be as good as him. But I would say, overall, Billy is better than Alfie."

"Yeah, he's always been a bit shy," Chloe agreed. "That said, he doesn't stop running, I've never met another player who works as hard as he does."

For the next few minutes, Chloe and

Reuben continued to debate the merits of both Billy and Alfie as footballers. So lost in conversation did the two friends become, that soon it was as though they had entirely forgotten that Jasper was even there.

This suited the other boy perfectly. Jasper's job was done. He was more than happy to do nothing more than listen.

Chapter thirteen

For the second day in a row, Alfie could barely believe what he was seeing. Yesterday he had been shocked to spot Jasper walking into school beside Hayden and Reuben. Today he was equally amazed to observe his nemesis strolling merrily past the school gates alongside Reuben and Chloe. Just what was going on?

He knew, just knew, that Jasper was attempting to stir trouble. The problem, though, was that he didn't know quite how.

It was something Alfie was going to have to find out soon. But for the time being it would have to wait. Right now he only wanted to find Billy.

Yet his best friend was nowhere to be found.

He had texted Billy three times the previous evening to try and arrange walking to school with him. The messages had gone unanswered. He'd then phoned him. Twice. Both times the calls went straight to voicemail.

Instead, Alfie decided to just call in at Billy's house on his way to school. They could walk in together from there.

However, this plan had also ended in failure.

Having slept through his alarm four times, and then ignored the many calls from his parents to 'get out of bed', Alfie had ended up leaving his house far later than he had meant to. Too late to be able to get to Billy's house before his buddy left for school. After getting dressed in record time, and briefly introducing his teeth to his toothbrush, he had dashed out of his house without so much as pausing to say good morning to his Mum, Dad or sister. He hadn't had any breakfast. He hadn't even styled his hair! This meant his tousled blond locks resembled a lion's mane. But Alfie didn't care. He just wanted to catch up with Billy.

Bizarrely, Alfie was in such a hurry to get to school, that he ended up arriving outside the gates 15 minutes earlier than he usually did. Quickly, he ran into the school; checked the common room, then rushed along the corridor to inspect Billy's tutor group classroom. There was no sign of him anywhere.

Satisfied that this meant his friend had not yet arrived at school, Alfie made his way back to the main gates to wait for him there.

The minutes ticked by. Alfie saw Liam. Then Daisy. Then Reuben, Chloe and Jasper. But not Billy. More time passed. Alfie heard the loud clanging of the first bell. The warning that it was time for all children to start making their way to their tutor groups. If you weren't in your classroom by the second bell then you were classed as late, and more often than not this meant only one thing. Detention.

Momentarily, Alfie debated giving Billy a little bit longer to show up. Then, sensibly deciding that the risk of suffering a detention simply wasn't worth it, he reluctantly made his way towards class. He figured Billy was either running late or, more likely, wasn't coming in again today.

He would be able to find out which of these two options was correct easily enough. Although, the two boys weren't in any of the same classes together, Liam was in Billy's tutor group. Liam was also in Alfie's maths class, and maths was the first lesson of the day.

Usually, Alfie despised maths. Especially algebra. He couldn't get his head round that. Couldn't for one moment understand why maths questions had letters in them as well as numbers. It made his brain ache! At least this morning, though, he would learn something useful from the lesson. He'd learn whether Billy was at school or not.

He really hoped that he was. Since his frustrating phone conversation with Madam Zola the previous evening, Alfie had been replaying the fortune teller's words in an almost constant loop inside his head. Well, the ones that he was able to hear, at least.

"I know you're trying your best to encourage Billy to play football again. Well done for that. Keep trying, but don't push too hard. The most important thing right now is that you're there for him. It's when we're feeling down that we need our friends the most."

Alfie was sure that Madam Zola was

urging him to be a better friend to Billy. That he needed to do more to try and cheer up his long-time best mate. He was still certain that the best way to lift his friend's spirits was by getting him to play football again.

He'd come so close to achieving this goal yesterday lunchtime. Alfie was certain that Billy had been just about to join in the lunchtime game. One more step and he would have been there, on the pitch, ready to dazzle everyone with his sublime skills.

Only Billy hadn't taken that final step. Instead he had just turned and walked the other way. Close. But not quite close enough.

Still, surely only a little further persuasion was required!

The problem, of course, was that Alfie had promised Billy he would not mention football to him again for the foreseeable future. He was also conscious of Madam Zola's warning not to push his friend too hard.

After much deliberation, Alfie believed he had come up with the perfect solution. Albeit, one that he would preferably not have had to have taken. Inside his school bag he had the very copy of FIFA that he had retrieved from Billy's rubbish sack a couple of days earlier. He was going to return this to his friend, explaining that he didn't feel right taking what, until a few days ago, had been the other boys favourite game.

Not only would this act as a way of getting Billy to think about football, without actually bringing the subject up, it was also a kind gesture. The sort of thing that only the very kindest friend would do. It was a win-win situation.

Now all he needed to do was find Billy.

Chapter fourteen

Encouragingly, Alfie discovered through Liam that Billy was indeed in school today.

Although he was somewhat surprised to hear that his best friend hadn't been late. In fact, according to Liam, Billy had already been sitting in the common room when he got there.

'He must have been in the toilet when I checked,' Alfie mused. 'I must have just missed him.'

Not that it really mattered. Billy was in school. That was the important thing. He'd just have to catch up with him at break-time.

Yet when break-time came, Alfie was still unable to find him. He checked in the common room; the playing fields; the canteen; he even popped into a couple of different toilets. There was no sign of Billy anywhere.

Toward the end of break-time, Alfie spotted Daisy and Chloe strolling in the direction of the science block. He sprinted over to his girlfriend to ask her whether she had seen his best friend. She had. He was in the common room.

"When?" Alfie demanded. "I've already looked in there!"

"Calm down, Alfie," Daisy gasped, clearly taken aback by the ferocity of her boyfriend's response. "He was there just now. We've just come from there."

Sheepishly, Alfie thanked Daisy, gave her a quick peck on the cheek, then looked briefly at Chloe. For a moment, he considered asking her why she had been walking alongside Jasper earlier that morning. He swiftly decided against doing so. He didn't have the time right now. He only wanted to find Billy.

Alfie pelted down the corridor and up the flight of stairs leading to the common room as fast as he could, barely bothering to dodge between the hordes of children coming the other way.

Arriving breathless at the common room

half-a-minute later, Alfie let out a wild howl of frustration. The room was empty. Everyone was already making their way towards their next class. He must have just missed him. Again! He couldn't believe his luck. Well, his lack of it.

It was a similar story at lunchtime. He was supposed to be spending the hour-long lunch break with Daisy. Instead he spent it dashing around the school, dipping in and out of one room or another, desperately searching for Billy. Much to Daisy's obvious annoyance.

Nearly everyone he asked reported having seen Billy just seconds before. Yet whenever Alfie arrived at the destination where they had supposedly seen him, he wasn't there. A more paranoid person could have been forgiven for believing that all this was some great big jape at their expense.

By the time the bell rang to signal the end of lunch, Alfie had still not located his friend. This was becoming an unexpectedly difficult mission!

No matter. After school would be fine.

Alfie knew that Billy had science last thing on a Wednesday. That was ideal. Alfie had French. The languages block was the closest building to the school gates. The building where the science labs were housed was on the opposite side of the school. Alfie would definitely be able to reach the main gate before his friend. He would wait for him there.

As soon as the end-of-school bell rang, Alfie gathered up his pencil case and work book, shoved it haphazardly into his bag, yanked his blazer off the back of his chair and hurried towards the exit. His teacher had barely dismissed the class by the time Alfie was through the door. There was no way he was going to miss Billy this time.

Unsurprisingly, Alfie was the first pupil to reach the school gates. He'd been waiting there for around five minutes when the first children he recognised from Billy's science class began to walk by him. Excellent. He would be there soon.

Except he wasn't.

Fifteen minutes later, Alfie was still standing by the school gates. The last trickle of Tideway School children ambled past him, talking excitedly about their plans for the evening ahead. Billy wasn't among them.

He waited another five minutes. There were now no longer any other children in sight. Guessing that Billy might have got a detention, Alfie jogged quickly over to his tutor room. The only person in the room was Mr Gumble, Billy's form tutor. Mr Gumble stated that Billy had not been in detention. No one had.

Alfie scratched his head. He must have missed him again. But how?

Shaking off his annoyance, Alfie slung his bag over his shoulder and once again began to sprint. This time in the direction of Billy's house. The pursuit of his friend was certainly helping to keep him fit.

He was just approaching the turning into the road where Billy lived, when he finally glimpsed his friend for the first time that day.

"Billy," Alfie yelled at the top of his voice. The other boy didn't respond. Didn't even flinch. Just carried on walking towards his house. "Bill," Alfie screamed again, even louder this time. Once again, his friend continued his determined march home.

Assuming that Billy was wearing his ear-phones and listening to music, Alfie gave up shouting and concentrated on running.

As he got closer he could see that Billy wasn't wearing any earphones. He tried shouting again to attract his friend's attention. The other boy still carried on walking.

Billy had just arrived at his front gate when Alfie finally caught up with him. "Billy," Alfie panted. "I've been looking for you everywhere."

Slowly, the other boy turned to face him. Alfie was instantly shocked to see the expression of disgust present on his best friend's face. He had never before seen him look so angry.

"I know," Billy hissed.

"You do?" Alfie replied, clearly surprised. "Then why didn't you come and find me. I've been all over the school looking for you. I've just been waiting by the gates for ages. Where have you…"

"Do you not get the hint, Alf?" Billy snapped venomously. "I don't want to talk to you right now. Just leave me alone, okay!"

Alfie's eyes opened wide. He was startled by the anger – almost hatred – in the other boy's voice. And expression. The boy with whom he had been very best friends for as long as he could remember. "But…"

"No buts, Alfie. Just leave me alone."

Billy turned to walk through his gate.

Alfie was just about to let him go, when he suddenly thrust his hand onto his friend's shoulder and forcibly turned him round so they were face-to-face once again.

"Not until you tell me what I've done wrong." His voice quivered with emotion. Alfie looked pleadingly into his best friend's eyes. Desperate to hear him say that he was only messing around. That this was all one big joke.

Effortlessly shrugging Alfie's hand off his shoulder, Billy made as if to walk away again, then stopped. He took a deep breath and began to speak. "You just can't ever leave anything alone, can you Alfie?" he bellowed angrily. "I told you the other night that I was done with football. That I wasn't interested anymore. Then what happens? I come into school yesterday to find that you've organised a match at lunchtime to try and get me to play. Oh, don't try to deny it. Hayden told me it was his idea, but I know it was yours. Hayden's never had an idea in his life!"

Usually, this would be the sort of quip that would make Alfie roar with laughter. Laughing was currently the furthest thing from his mind, though.

"A few weeks ago, I played for Kingsway

United's Academy against last season's Premier League champions," Billy continued, his level of anger continuing to rise. "Why would I want to waste my time playing in a lunchtime kickabout? I'm better than that. Or, at least, I thought I was."

Alfie tried to speak. Tried to reassure his best friend that he was still good enough. That his dream wasn't necessarily over. But Billy didn't give him a chance to speak. Just carried on talking, his voice becoming ever more scornful.

"You know, after you'd left my house the other night I went over to that bag of rubbish in my room. I was going to get that FIFA game out and give it to you at school. And what do I find? You've already taken it! You must have been really upset for me, Alf. But, hey, at least you got something out of it, didn't you?"

"But..." Alfie cried. He swung his bag from his shoulder, and began fumbling with its zip, desperate to show Billy that he had been about to return the game.

But Billy still wasn't interested in anything Alfie had to say to him. "Do you know what the worst thing is?" he asked, his voice suddenly so quiet that it took

Alfie a second or two to realise he'd been asked a question.

"W... what?" Alfie stuttered. He cursed under his breath as the zip on his bag snagged against some material, rendering him temporarily unable to open it.

"The worst thing," Billy repeated, just as Alfie stopped wrestling with his bag as the zip finally came free... "is that I'm a much better player than you. Always have been. And everyone knows it. They all say it. Yet you're the one that's in a professional team's academy." He paused, then sighed miserably. "It's just so unfair."

Alfie reeled backwards as if he had been struck. Violently stung by Billy's cruel words. They hurt far more than a punch ever could.

Before he could recover from the shock, Billy turned into his garden, opened the front door and slammed it shut so hard that it caused the glass panes to rattle.

Alfie was left standing alone on the pavement. Clinging hopelessly to his former best friend's copy of FIFA.

Chapter fifteen

It was Megan who called Daisy. She had never before seen her brother look so distraught.

The sight of his face the moment he had walked through the front door that afternoon had instantly stirred in her a new sensation. One she had not thought it was possible to feel when it came to her older sibling. Sympathy.

Tentatively, she had asked Alfie if he had finished with Daisy. His response? 'Get lost Moggy. I'm not in the mood.' From that moment on he had shut himself away in his bedroom, only briefly emerging at tea-time in order to collect his dinner plate before promptly disappearing back into the safety of his bedroom to eat it there. He had made it very clear to Megan and his parents that he wished to be left alone.

Yet Megan did not want to leave him alone. She could tell something was wrong. Badly wrong. After a few more unsuccessful attempts to find out what had upset her brother so much she decided to take matters into her own hands.

Normally, Megan wouldn't bother to interfere in Alfie's personal life. It just wasn't worth the hassle. Sure, it was fun winding him up about his relationship with Daisy. In fact, it was practically her hobby. Yet directly involving herself in it... she wouldn't do that. Or so she thought.

Soon after finishing her pudding, Megan had rushed up to her bedroom, trying desperately to remember where she had left her phone. She had only had it for two weeks. It had been a present for her eleventh birthday. She had been desperate for one. Had been pleading with Mr and Mrs Jones to buy her one for months. Explaining that all her friends had one. She needed one. Owning a phone would make her life complete.

In the two weeks that she had actually

owned the phone, Megan had spent more time trying to remember where she had left it than she had actually using it. When she did use it, she tended to spend most of her time watching music videos of her favourite pop groups on YouTube. When she wasn't doing that, she was normally playing games on it.

Bizarrely, one thing she didn't tend to do with the phone, was actually use it to talk to her friends.

In fact, aside from a couple of calls to her grandparents, and one to her home phone to check it worked properly, she hadn't actually called any of her friends on it. Not once. Until now.

Unbeknown to Alfie, Megan had copied some of his friend's numbers onto her phone. Including Daisy's. She never really planned to call any of these secretly obtained numbers. Yet she wanted to have more people's numbers on her phone than any of her friends did on theirs. It had become something of a badge of honour among the Year 6 children at the Kingsway Junior School to have as many 'friend' contact details as possible. Okay, so half the contacts on the phone weren't actually her friends. Who cared? No one else would ever know.

Eventually, after a few minutes of searching, Megan located her phone underneath a pile of magazines that were scattered at the foot of her bed. She brought up her contacts list, found Daisy's name, and called her.

Daisy didn't usually answer calls from numbers that she didn't recognise. However, just as she had been about to reject the call, she had a sudden change of heart. She had been trying to ring Alfie for most of the afternoon. Yet his phone continually went straight to voicemail. This was odd. Outside of school hours, Alfie's phone was very rarely switched off.

Therefore, instead of ignoring the unknown number, she had considered it might be Alfie ringing from a friend's phone so decided to answer it.

She was glad she did. As was Megan.

After an awkward start to the conversation, whereby Megan had had to explain who it was that was calling and why she was ringing (she declined to say how and why she had the other girl's number), it was quickly established that Daisy had not finished her relationship with Alfie. At least, not as far as she was aware.

Megan then explained to Daisy about

how Alfie had come home from school in a foul mood. Far worse than anything she had ever seen before. She even admitted to Daisy that she was worried about her brother. "Please don't tell Alfie I said that," Megan had then begged, causing Alfie's girlfriend to chuckle.

Ultimately, the two girls agreed that Daisy stood the best chance of getting any information out of Alfie. There was no way he would speak to Megan, and even less chance he would open up to their parents. It was Daisy or no one.

Having checked with her Mum to make sure that she was allowed to pop round Alfie's house for an hour or two, Daisy told Megan that she would be there as soon as possible. Half-an-hour later, both girls were standing outside Alfie's bedroom door.

Having knocked on the door a few times, and not received a response, Daisy decided enough was enough. Gesturing for Megan to leave her to it, she gently knocked one final time, then slowly pushed down the handle and slipped quietly into the room, closing the door firmly shut behind her.

Megan had not been exaggerating. Alfie looked terrible. He was lying on his bed staring forlornly up at the ceiling. His dinner remained untouched on his bedside table. She could instantly tell from the puffiness around his eyes that he had been crying. She had never seen him cry before.

"Alfie, what's wrong?" Daisy asked, the concern clearly audible in her voice.

It seemed to take the boy a moment or two to realise that there was someone else in the room with him. Then, slowly, he turned his head, ever so slightly, towards her. "Daisy," he said, sounding surprised. "What are you doing here?"

For a moment, Daisy was about to tell him about Megan's phone call. Then, remembering what the younger girl had asked, she simply answered: "I've been trying to ring you. You didn't answer so I thought I'd call round to check that you're alright. Are you alright?"

For a good couple of minutes, Alfie refused to talk about what had upset him. He half-heartedly tried to convince his girlfriend that nothing was wrong. That he was just tired. Daisy didn't believe a word he said.

It was only when Daisy started to worry that she was the cause of his upset and admitted to being worried that he wanted to end their relationship, that Alfie finally opened up about his earlier encounter with Billy.

By the time he had finished recalling the events from a few hours earlier, he was on the verge of tears again.

Daisy walked over to the bed and sat down next to him. She put her arm around him and tenderly rested her on head his left shoulder. "He's just upset, Alfie. I'm sure he didn't mean what he said."

Slowly, Alfie shook his head, as though his girlfriend didn't fully understand what he was saying. "But what if he's right?" he asked, his voice flat. "What if I'm really not good enough to be in an Academy. I remember reading somewhere, in one of my Kick-Off magazines I think, that something like only 180 of around 1.5 million children playing youth football will make it as a pro. Let's face it, what chance have I got?"

"As much chance as anyone else, Alfie," Daisy answered encouragingly. "Look, you know that I don't know much about football. Anything in fact. But I know that you're good. You wouldn't be in an Academy if you weren't. Chloe told me once that you're one of the hardest working, most dedicated players that she knows. Surely that must count for something."

"But I'm not as good as Billy," Alfie whined, not taking one bit of encouragement from Daisy's words. "He's better than me and even he probably won't make it. I've got absolutely no chance."

Daisy removed her head from Alfie's shoulder, then used her hands to turn his face so that his eyes were looking directly into hers.

"Maybe you're actually a better player than Billy." she said. "Maybe that's why you're still in an Academy and he's not. Maybe you need to have a bit more confidence in your own ability."

These final words seem to have some effect on Alfie. After all, they were almost exactly the same ones that he had heard Madam Zola, Noel Forint and Matty Simmons say to him over the past few days.

"But..." Alfie began, albeit with slightly less conviction than before. "But... everyone knows he's better than me."

"Who's everyone, Alfie? Billy was upset when he said what he did. He didn't mean it. I promise you."

Alfie nodded thoughtfully. Yet before he could reply, a sudden dinging sound halted their conversation. It took Alfie a moment or two to comprehend what the sound was. Then he realised. An email had come through on his laptop computer which was, as ever, left open on a small desk underneath the room's window.

He glanced at the screen. He didn't recognise the sender. Importantnews@outlookmail1.co.uk. Initially, he ignored it, convinced it was probably just spam or junk mail. Then he noticed the email's subject line. Alfie, you really need to hear this.

Without so much as another word to Daisy, Alfie made his way over to the computer and opened the email.

He knew instantly who it was from.

Chapter sixteen

Ten minutes later, Alfie slumped back onto his bed. Devastated. Nothing that Daisy said could make him feel any better. Not that he was listening to a word she said anyway.

Instead, he just kept replaying the words he'd just heard over and over in his mind. His worst fears had been confirmed. What Billy had told him earlier that afternoon was indeed true. Everyone really did think that Billy was a better player than him. Including his closest friends.

Alfie had known that the mysterious email would have come from Madam Zola. It was exactly the kind of thing that she would do in order to attract his attention. He had clicked on the first of the three attachments that were included within the email full of hope and anticipation. Certain that the fortune teller was sending him a message that would explain just what he had to do to rebuild his friendship with Billy.

What he actually heard shocked him to the core.

First came Hayden's voice: *"I suppose Billy is a bit better. I mean Alfie is still really good, but when he's on form, Billy can be class. Some of his skills are ridiculously good!"*

Then Chloe's: *"When I played for the Colts, Billy was much better than anyone else in the team. At least until Hayden started playing. They were both as good as each other."*

And finally, Reuben's: *"If he believed in himself a bit more then he could probably be as good as him. But I would say, overall, Billy is better than Alfie."*

There was no mistaking the voices. The recordings were as clear as a bell. Three of his closest friends all agreeing that Billy was a better footballer than he was.

He felt angry and betrayed.

Yet there was a part of him – a small part, but a part nevertheless – that couldn't help but agree with what he had just heard.

After all, didn't he himself believe that Billy was a better footballer? Why would his friends feel any differently? Facts were facts. Not that this made their assessments seem any less hurtful.

The more he thought about it, the more he came to the same conclusion. His friends all thought he was lucky to be in an Academy. Especially now Billy was no longer in one. Worse still, the more he thought about it, the more he tended to agree with them.

If there was one thing Alfie really couldn't understand, it was why Madam Zola had sent him the email in the first place.

Normally everything the fortune teller did she did for a reason. No matter how strange that reason seemed at the time. Her actions were meant to help him towards his ultimate goal. His dream. His destiny. To one day become a professional footballer.

Yet how could hearing his friends happily admit that he wasn't as good as his best friend – his best friend that was no longer in an Academy – possibly help him? Was he supposed to break his friendships in order to keep his dream alive? If so, why had Madam Zola previously been so keen for him to help Billy? It just didn't make any sense.

He needed to speak to the fortune teller as quickly as possible. Yet he knew only too well from past experience that Madam Zola would only contact him when she was ready to. And even then, he probably wouldn't get the answers he was looking for.

So lost in thought was Alfie, that he'd almost completely forgotten that Daisy was still in the room with him. It was only when his girlfriend prodded him quite stiffly in the ribs, that he suddenly remembered that she was present.

"Ouch. That hurt," he moaned.

"Sorry," Daisy replied. "I have been trying to get your attention for ages, though. I've just texted Chloe and got a reply. She denies that she said Billy's better than you. She said…"

"Well that's clearly a lie," Alfie roared, before Daisy could finish her sentence. He sat bolt upright and fixed his girlfriend with a hard stare. The girl flinched, taken aback by the sudden anger in her boyfriend's voice. "I'm sorry. I didn't mean to shout," he continued, adopting a softer, yet still stern tone. "But you heard what she said with your own ears. There's no point in her denying it. She said what she said, and that's that.

"Yes, but..." Daisy began again, only to once more be cut off by Alfie.

"Look, I don't want to be rude but I just want to be alone right now," he said. "It's probably time you should be getting home anyway. It's getting late.

"But... Alfie..."

"Please Daisy. Just leave." The words came out sounding far more demanding than he had meant them to.

Without offering her boyfriend a hug, or even saying goodbye, Daisy stood up, marched straight over to the door, opened it and strode through.

"Daisy, I'm sorry. I didn't mean..." Alfie croaked. But it was too late. Before he could finish his apology, Daisy had already slammed his bedroom door firmly shut. He could hear her footsteps echo down the hallway. They paused briefly, he guessed outside Megan's bedroom, then started up again a moment or two later. He heard the familiar creak of the fourth step as she made her way down the stairs, then muffled voices as Daisy said goodnight to his parents. The next sound was of the front door opening and closing. Then silence.

Momentarily, Alfie considered going after her. He quickly decided against doing so. He couldn't handle another confrontation. Not right now. There was just too much going on in his head. He needed time to think. He would make it up to Daisy in the morning. Hopefully.

He had just settled back down on to his bed, when he heard his parents calling for him to come downstairs. He had been expecting this. No doubt they would want to know why Daisy had stormed out only moments after they'd heard him shouting.

Yet more hassle that he didn't need.

It was while he was making his way dejectedly downstairs to face his parents, that Alfie began to seriously consider doing something he'd never thought of doing before. Something that up until that point he would never have dreamed of even thinking about.

But as he thought about his arguments with Daisy and Billy, the hurt caused by his friends seemingly not believing in him and the doubts he possessed that he would ever really be good enough to make it as a professional footballer, the more convinced he became that he should follow Billy's lead.

Maybe it was time for Alfie Jones to quit playing football.

Thursday

Chapter seventeen

Jasper Johnson could have danced with joy.

The previous evening he had started to doubt whether his plan would actually work. His finger had hesitated over his computer's mouse. Was it really worth clicking send?

What was the point of launching the email into the realms of cyberspace? It was more than likely that it would only end up in the recipients' junk mail folder anyway, forever to remain unseen.

Even if it didn't, what were the chances of Alfie actually opening it? They were always being told at school to never open emails from addresses they didn't recognise. Would Alfie heed this advice, or would curiosity get the better of him?

His finger had wavered over the mouse for what seemed like an eternity. Eventually, he had decided to take a chance. To just go for it. He'd come too far with his plan to give up now. If it didn't work, he would just have to think of another way to get Alfie to listen to the special messages he had for him. There was always another way.

Jasper had taken a deep breath, and then brought his finger down firmly onto the mouse button. The email had been sent. He crossed his fingers. Hoping beyond hope that the email would find its intended target.

Strolling into school that Thursday morning, it quickly became apparent that Alfie had opened the email. One glance at his nemesis's miserable face confirmed that. As Alfie trudged despondently past the school gates there was no doubting that Alfie was upset about something.

More tellingly, he was alone. Alfie hardly ever walked to school by himself. If he wasn't with Daisy, he'd be with Billy. If he wasn't with either of them he would be with Hayden and Reuben, sometimes even Liam or Chloe. Even on the rare occasions that he did walk to school by himself, he would always wait by the gates to meet his friends.

Today, though, he didn't stop to wait for anyone. Just plodded into school. Totally alone. Lost in thought.

Had he looked up, he would almost certainly have noticed Jasper leaning against some railings no more than a couple of strides away from him. He would have realised that the larger boy was staring intently at him, a beaming smile lighting up his round, red face.

This would surely have given Alfie cause to be suspicious. A clue that Jasper, not Madam Zola, was behind the mysterious email he had received. But Alfie didn't look up. Not once. A marching band could have marched by, blaring out a whole medley of tunes. Alfie wouldn't have noticed. He was totally pre-occupied.

Moments after Alfie had passed by, Jasper noticed Billy walking towards the gates. He too looked utterly miserable. The dour expression on Billy's face only served to widen Jasper's smile. If it was to get any wider he would be in serious danger of his face splitting in two.

Yet Jasper knew he had to remove the smile from his face for the time being. He wanted to talk to Billy. He didn't want to be grinning like a maniac as he did so.

"Morning Billy," Jasper called cheerfully as his prey approached.

The other boy briefly looked up, saw who had shouted his name, then carried on walking.

Realising that the other boy wasn't going to acknowledge him, Jasper took a step away from the railings to position himself right in front of Billy. His sheer bulk made it impossible for Billy to pass.

"What do you want, Jasper?" Billy asked moodily, as Jasper's imposing shadow fell across his path.

"I was just wondering how you're doing after... you know... the whole Kingsway United thing," Jasper replied. He sounded so concerned that even Jasper himself was starting to believe he was being genuine. There could be no doubt that he was certainly starting to nail the whole acting malarkey.

"I'm fine," Billy snapped. "Why do you care so much anyway? We're not friends Jasper. We never have been. Never will be. Now leave me alone."

Bowing his head and fixing his saddest expression to his face, Jasper shuffled to one side to allow Billy past. "Fine," he sighed sadly. "I'm just trying to help.

I've been there, remember. I know what you're going through." He let Billy take a couple of steps past him. Then, as innocently as he could, said: "Alfie's just arrived by the way. About two minutes before you got here."

Immediately, Billy stopped in his tracks. He turned to face Jasper. "I couldn't care less whether Alfie's here or not," he snarled. "I've got nothing to say to him either." With that, he spun on his heels and marched purposely past the school gates.

The moment he was out of view, Jasper let out a whoop of delight. He didn't care who heard him. He was simply ecstatic. Finally, after many years of trying, one of his plans was working. He was actually making Alfie's life miserable. Revenge was sweet. Far sweeter than Jasper had ever dreamed it would be.

Even the sight of Chloe Reed advancing towards him with a face like thunder couldn't dampen his spirits. He had fully expected to be confronted by her today. Out of the three people whose voices he had recorded, Jasper knew that Chloe was the one who was most likely to work out what had happened. Even if Hayden and Reuben had figured it out, Jasper doubted they would have approached him. They would have been too scared. Jasper's sheer size made him an intimidating presence. Very few people ever dared to stand up to him. Chloe was one of the few who did.

"I know what you've done, Jasper," she yelled as she drew closer. The volume of her voice caused a whole host of other children to stop what they were doing and stare at the commotion. Noticing that whatever was going on involved the gigantic form of Jasper Johnson, the majority decided to swiftly carry on with their own plans.

"I don't know what you mean," Jasper answered, raising both his hands as if to demonstrate his innocence.

"Don't play dumb with me," Chloe snarled. "I know all about the message you sent to Alfie. You must have recorded our conversation on the phone, then somehow edited the bits you needed." She was now standing directly in front of Jasper. The size difference between the two teenagers was stark. Chloe was more than a full head shorter than the boy. Yet she wasn't at all daunted by him.

"I really don't know what you're..." Jasper began, attempting to maintain his display of innocence. He couldn't do it, though. He found the look of disgust on Chloe's face just too funny to be able to keep up the act.

Instead he burst into a fit of a laughter. The familiar evil smirk instantly returned to his features. "Oh, you should see your face," Jasper said, once he'd finished laughing. "You do look ever so serious. Does Alfie not like you anymore?" He asked the question in the most mocking tone he could muster.

"You won't get away with this, Jasper," Chloe continued, trying her hardest not to give the boy the satisfaction he craved by reacting to his jibe. "Once we explain to Alfie what's happened, once he knows it's you that's behind all this, he'll..."

"He'll what? Forgive you?" Jasper asked, snidely. "I think that's where your wrong, Chloe. Okay, so he'll know that I sent the message. So what? He doesn't like me and I don't like him. It's not our friendship that will be affected. Yet no matter who sent the message, that doesn't change what you said. You, Hayden and Reuben all admitted to me that Billy is better than him. And now he's heard you say it."

"But there was more to the conversation to that. You tricked us."

Jasper was just about to proudly admit to the fact, when something stopped him from doing so. A sudden thought occurred to him. Chloe could be using her phone to record him, much in the same way he had each of them.

Instead he shrugged his shoulders. "I don't remember tricking anyone. You said what you said and Alfie's heard you. Judging by how he looked this morning, he won't be forgiving any of you any time soon."

"You won't get away with this, Jasper," Chloe repeated, although this time the words didn't sound as certain as they had a moment before. As much as she hated to admit it, Jasper had made some good points.

"We'll see," said Jasper, giving Chloe a wink that made her flesh crawl. "But I very much doubt Alfie will listen to another word you have to say anytime soon."

Any further conversation was swiftly halted by the sound of the first bell. Without another word, Jasper cockily swung his bag over his shoulder, gave a Chloe an exaggerated wave goodbye and then sauntered merrily towards school, whistling tunelessly as he went.

Frustratedly, Chloe reached into the pocket of her school blazer, pulled out her phone and switched its voice recorder off. She had been hopeful that Jasper would have admitted that there was more to the conversations than he had sent. She was sure that he had been about to before something had stopped him. He must have gotten suspicious. Begrudgingly, Chloe had to admit that Jasper was becoming more devious the older he got.

Yet something the large boy had said had got her thinking. While he was right that Alfie was unlikely to listen to anything she, Hayden or Reuben had to say, there was one person that Chloe was fairly sure her friend would listen to.

Chapter eighteen

That school day had been one of the strangest of Alfie's life. He had spent the entire duration of its break and lunch times looking for Daisy and Billy, whilst simultaneously trying to avoid Chloe, Reuben and Hayden. He had nothing to say to any of those three and wasn't interested in hearing their excuses.

Fortunately, he was not due to be in the same class as any of the treacherous trio that day. Avoiding them had therefore proved fairly simple.

Unfortunately, his mission to locate the other two had proved rather more problematic.

Billy, as had been the case the previous day, was nowhere to be found. In truth,

Alfie hadn't held out much hope of finding him, but had resolved to try anyway. He was desperate to make amends with his former best friend. So desperate, that he was fully prepared to tell Billy that he would give up playing football if this would somehow help to rebuild their shattered friendship.

Yet Billy was seemingly something of a master at staying out of sight. Alfie had never realised that the boy he had been so close to for so many years was such an expert at hide-and-seek. Well, the hiding part anyway.

His attempts to find Daisy had proved equally fruitless. If anything, he was even more keen to find Daisy than he was Billy. He wanted – needed – to apologise to his girlfriend. He hadn't meant to snap at her. He knew she was only trying to help. Yet every time he caught a glimpse of her she was with Chloe; and there was no way Alfie was going anywhere near her. Not yet. Not ever!

On his way to school that morning, Alfie had considered texting Daisy. Not to apologise. That was something he felt he needed to do face-to-face. But to arrange to meet up with her somewhere, alone; or at least away from Chloe.

For the first time since his unpleasant altercation with Billy, he had turned his phone on, fully intending to text her. Yet the moment it had booted up, he was met with a flurry of beeps and bings. Each one informing him of an incoming message. There were hundreds of them.

He quickly noted that they were all from either Chloe, Hayden or Reuben. No doubt trying to apologise for what he had heard them say. Maybe even denying that they'd even said it. Alfie, didn't care what any of those messages said. He simply turned his phone back off. If he wanted to speak to Daisy, then he'd just have to be patient and wait until she was alone.

It was now 16:30 and he still hadn't managed to speak to her. He'd waited at the school gates for her, but had had to scarper when he saw Reuben and Hayden heading meaningfully in his direction.

Twenty minutes later, he was at her front door, hoping that she would have come straight home from school. He was out of luck. Mrs Saunders informed him that Daisy had called to say that she was going to the park with Chloe and some of her other friends. She expressed surprise that Alfie wasn't with them, then invited him in to wait for her. He declined. Alfie

didn't know how much Daisy's Mum
knew about their falling out, if anything.
He didn't feel like hanging around to find
out. Politely thanking her for the offer,
Alfie made his excuses and left.

He was plodding in the direction
of the park when he heard it. That
unmistakable sound. The one that he
knew so well.

Initially he was convinced his ears were
playing tricks on him. He never got this
lucky. Ever. What's more, he knew that
his phone was turned off. There was
simply no way the sound could be real.

Except it was. It really was.

T-ting-a-ching. T-ting-a-ching. T-ting-a-
ching.

Excitedly, Alfie plunged his left hand
into his blazer pocket and yanked out his
phone. Sure enough, there on the screen,
looking directly back at him, was Madam
Zola.

"I'm so glad you've called," Alfie
jabbered elatedly at the screen. "I really
need to ask you..."

He paused. There was something about
the fortune teller's face that made him
stop talking. She looked angry. Incredibly
angry. Her brown eyes blazed with fury
and her usually welcoming expression

had been replaced by a scowl that made her wrinkled face look like that of an angry bulldog.

"How can you have been so stupid, Alfie?" she asked scornfully. "How can you have been such a... such a nitwit?"

This was totally out of character. He had never seen or heard Madam Zola so irate before. "What... what do you mean?" he stammered in response.

"What do I mean?" cried Madam Zola. "What do I mean? I'll tell you what I mean. I warned you, Alfie. Warned you that someone was trying to stir trouble. Yet you were so blinded by anger. By stupidity. By your own selfishness... that you didn't see it. Even though it was so obvious. I'm so very disappointed with you. I really am."

"What do you..." Alfie started to repeat the same question he had just asked. Then stopped. Suddenly it hit him. Like running into a goalpost at full speed. How could he have been so stupid? "The email," he groaned. "It wasn't from you. It was from Jasper."

Immediately upon hearing Alfie say the words, Madam Zola's expression softened. She instantly appeared more like the friendly fortune teller he was so used to.

"Of course the email wasn't from me," she acknowledged. "Why would you ever think it was?"

"Well, to be fair, it is exactly the kind of thing you'd do."

Madam Zola shrugged her shoulders, but didn't respond further.

"To be honest, I'm not sure the fact that the message didn't come from you makes any difference," Alfie continued, after a short pause for thought. "I mean... it doesn't really matter who sent the email. It doesn't change anything. Not really. The fact is, three of my closest friends all think Billy is a better football player than me. And, do you know what? I think they are probably right. He is. If Billy can't make it, what chance have I got?"

"Alfie," Madam Zola replied softly. Her voice was now barely louder than a whisper. "We've spoken about this already. About your need to have more belief in yourself. I'm here to help you achieve your destiny. But it can only come true if you listen to what I have to say, and right now I'm telling you that you need to have more confidence in your ability. Confidence is one of, if not, the most important asset that any professional footballer possesses. Without it, you're right. You don't stand much chance."

"Yeah, well," Alfie continued. "I've been thinking about that. Maybe everything that's happened this week is trying to tell me something. That this is all just a childish dream. I've lost my best friend, possibly my girlfriend as well, and fallen out with three other good mates. All over football. Maybe all this just isn't worth it."

Briefly, a flash of anger returned to Madam Zola's eyes. It passed as quickly as it had arrived. "I don't for one moment think you really believe that, Alfie," she said, continuing with her gentle tone. "I've already told you that Billy will come round given time. I promise you. You just need to be patient. He's hurting at the moment. His reaction is quite common. Lots of young boys rejected or released by academies react this way. They quit football. Lash out at friends and family. It's not fair they feel this way. It's not their fault. But it's the way it is. Your dream isn't over, though, Alfie. Not if you don't want it to be. As for Chloe, Hayden and Reuben... why don't you just talk to them. Listen to what they have to say?"

The teenager thought for a moment.

"Because I don't know if I can trust them anymore," he answered sadly.

Madam Zola frowned at the boy's response. Then glanced down at her wrist. Needless to say, she wasn't wearing a watch. "I need to be going, Alfie. Things to do, people to see. You know how it is. Just promise me that you'll think carefully about everything that I've just said."

"I will," Alfie promised.

"Oh, and one more thing." The fortune teller was speaking fast now, as if hurried. "You need to get home. Now!" Someone's waiting to speak to you. Go. Right away. It's important." The very second these final words left her lips, her vision disappeared instantly from the phone screen.

Alfie shook his head. A small smile graced his face. The fortune teller had certainly given him plenty to think about. Although he was still in no mood to confront either Chloe, Reuben or Hayden or listen to what they had to say.

Before returning his phone to his pocket, Alfie turned it on. He wanted to check whether Daisy had bothered to text him. Seconds later, a whole raft of beeps and tings filled the air as more unread messages appeared on his phone. Most came from the same trio. There were none from Daisy. There was, however, one from his Mum. Ignoring the other messages, Alfie scrolled down to that one and opened it.

'Can you come home ASAP. There's someone here to see you.'

Alfie's smile became a touch wider. You had to hand it to Madam Zola. She didn't often get things wrong.

Once more, Alfie turned off his phone. He put it back in his pocket, then began a gentle jog towards home.

He was hopeful, and fairly certain, that Daisy would be waiting for him when he got there.

He was wrong.

Chapter nineteen

The Jumper should have given it away.
Had Alfie been paying attention, he
would undoubtedly have noticed the thick
green woollen jumper that was hanging
in the hallway. The jumper that didn't
belong to Alfie, his sister or either of their
parents. Yet one that should have been
instantly recognisable.

But Alfie wasn't paying attention. He
was too busy concentrating on what he
would say to Daisy. So the jumper went
unnoticed.

Therefore, as Alfie raced into the living
room and saw that it wasn't actually
Daisy who was waiting for him, he
couldn't have felt more surprised.

"J... J... Jimmy," Alfie spluttered,

struggling to overcome the shock of seeing his first ever football coach sitting in his parents' front room.

Alfie hadn't seen Jimmy Grimshaw for over a year. Strangely enough, the last time he had seen him, the old man had been sat in the exact same seat. He couldn't have been certain, but Alfie was fairly sure that his former coach was even sipping tea from the exact same mug.

On that occasion, Jimmy had informed Alfie that there was a chance he would be offered a trial at the Kingsway United Academy. A chance that would disappear should Alfie agree to join the Norton Town Academy.

It had been an agonising choice. United were the team he supported and had long dreamed of playing for. Norton were a smaller club whose first team played in a lower division. What's more, the town of Norton was also located 60 miles away. Ultimately, however, Alfie had plumped to join the Norton Town Academy. Advice from Madam Zola had helped him reach that decision. But there was more to it than that. He simply felt more comfortable at Norton. More... wanted.

Given what had happened to Billy within the past week, Alfie couldn't help

but feel he had definitely made the right choice.

"Surprised?" Jimmy inquired in his usually calm tone of voice.

"You could say that," Alfie responded. His eyes never left the old man's face. A face that appeared to have grown even more wrinkles in the time since Alfie had last seen it. While Jimmy had always looked old to Alfie, he now looked ancient. He'd lost so much weight that his long face was skeleton thin; his cheek bones razor sharp. The teenager couldn't help but notice the old man's mottled hands shake dreadfully as he stretched to place his mug of tea on the coffee table. He couldn't believe how frail his old coach suddenly seemed. He didn't look at all well.

"I hear you're doing well at Norton Town," Jimmy continued, unable to hide the pride from his voice. The elderly coach was clearly not in any hurry to get to the purpose of his visit.

"Better than Billy's doing at United," Alfie spat. The reply was out of his mouth before he'd had a chance to engage his brain. He couldn't help it. The sight of Jimmy had instantly made Alfie think of his best friend. Or rather his ex-best friend. Jimmy was the head of Youth Development at Kingsway United. Surely he could have done more to keep Billy at the Academy? If Billy hadn't been released, then they would still be best friends. None of the past week's events would have taken place. In that moment, that split second, Alfie blamed his former coach for all of his current problems.

Jimmy winced at the fierceness of the boy's response. The pained expression on the old man's withered face instantly made Alfie regret the harsh tone he had used.

Before Jimmy could respond, Mrs Jones bustled into the front room, carrying a plate of biscuits. "Oh, Alfie you're home at last," she said, noting her son's presence. "Why did it take you so long to get home from school? Were you with Daisy? Or Billy? You weren't in detention, were you?" Mrs Jones's barrage of questions was suddenly halted as she observed the elderly visitors' face. "Are you okay, Jimmy?" she asked, clearly concerned by what she saw.

For a moment, the old man sat motionless. Rooted to the spot. Then, very slowly, he turned towards the boy's Mum. "Yes. I'm fine, thanks." He smiled, some of the usual warmth returning to his face.

Mrs Jones nodded uncertainly, then looked at Alfie. Her son just looked guilty. There was a moment of awkward silence. Then Alfie said, "Please go, Mum. We need to talk."

As requested, Mrs Jones made her way out of the living room, totally confused. She had assumed Alfie would have been delighted to see Jimmy. The tension that was clearly present in the room had been the last thing she had expected.

"Look, Jimmy," Alfie began once his Mum had shut the door behind her. "I'm sorry, I didn't mean what I just..."

The old man held up a hand to quieten

the boy. "It's okay, Alfie," he responded. "I know all about what's happened over the past week."

"How?" Alfie asked. Surely Jimmy didn't possess Madam Zola-like powers!

"Chloe phoned me last night," the old man admitted. "She told me everything."

Upon hearing Chloe's name mentioned, it took all of Alfie's willpower not to storm out of the front room. He didn't, though. He felt truly terrible about the way he had just snapped at the old man. A man that had always been so kind to him. Without Jimmy's help and encouragement over the years it was highly unlikely that he would be in an Academy today. Alfie knew it. He owed it to the elderly coach to stay and listen to what he had to say.

"I understand you must blame me for some of what's happened over the past week," Jimmy continued, as if reading the teenager's mind. "After all, it was my call to release Billy, wasn't it? I'm the Head of Youth Development at Kingsway United, aren't I?"

Alfie shrugged his shoulders. Then slowly nodded his head. "I guess," he agreed.

Jimmy smiled. But it wasn't a warm

smile. If anything, the smile somehow made the old man appear incredibly sad. "I wish I could have kept Billy on, Alfie," Jimmy stated, miserably shaking his head. "Agreeing to release Billy was one of the hardest things I've ever had to do in my life. I've known him, and you for that matter, since you were little boys. Now look at you. You're both nearly as tall as I am. The truth is, not one of the other coaches felt that Billy had progressed in the way that was expected of him over the past season. Don't get me wrong, they don't think he's suddenly become a bad player. But talent will only get you so far. Success is as much about attitude as talent. And determination. Unfortunately, the coaches just didn't feel Billy showed enough desire to make it to the next level.

"He wasn't the only one. Only five out of the twenty boys were kept on. I tried my best to sway their decision. But in the end, I had to listen to what my coaches were saying. They see him at every training session. At every match. I had to trust them to make the right decision."

The old man's words made Alfie think back to his own experiences inside the Norton Town dressing room that past

Sunday. In his mind, he clearly saw the image of some of his teammates – most of them, in fact – walking out of Matty Simmons' office on the brink of tears. Their bodies shaking uncontrollably as they battled to keep their emotions in check upon hearing the news that they had dreaded.

"Football is a great game," Jimmy continued. "It's often called the beautiful game. And it is a beautiful game. It can also, though, be a very cruel game. Especially for those young boys who aren't quite good enough to make it. To be brutally honest, that will be most of them."

Jimmy paused for a moment and looked steadily at Alfie. He wanted to make sure the teenager was listening carefully to what was being said. It was clear that he had the boy's undivided attention.

"But you, Alfie, you have a real chance of making it. You've always had the attitude and desire, and from what I see and hear you've got the talent now as well. Oh, don't look so surprised. Just because you're not in my Academy doesn't mean I don't keep tabs on you."

"Do... do you really think I can make it?" Alfie asked, doubtfully.

"Yes." There was no hesitation in the reply. Jimmy smiled again. This time, the smile lit up his skeletal features. He suddenly looked more like the Jimmy Alfie remembered. "I really do. And so do all your friends."

"Pah," Alfie scoffed. "I know that's not true. I've heard them all say that Billy's better than me. They're probably right," he added miserably.

Jimmy paused again, carefully weighing up his next words. "What you heard was what Jasper wanted you to hear," Jimmy began. "You know Jasper well enough to realise that there would have been far more to each of those conversations than the snippets you heard, don't you," he stated, rather than asked.

Alfie nodded reluctantly. "Yeah. Now I know that Jasper sent the email, I'm sure there is more to it. But it still doesn't change the fact that at some point during their conversation they still all admitted to thinking that Billy's better than me."

"Maybe he is more skilful than you," Jimmy mused. "Maybe he's quicker. Stronger. More agile."

"There's no maybe about it," Alfie sighed dejectedly. "He's all of those things."

"Yet as I've just told you," Jimmy carried

on, ignoring Alfie's sullenness. "There's more to making it as a professional footballer than talent alone. You need to be right in here and there," he added, using one hand to point to his heart, and the other to his head. "And you've got it Alfie. There's no doubt about it. You just need to believe it yourself. Remember, hard work beats talent, if talent doesn't work hard."

The room fell silent for a good few minutes. Alfie was completely lost in thought. Carefully thinking about everything that Jimmy had just said.

The silence was eventually ended by a loud creaking noise. Alfie glanced towards the window believing that a car must have just scraped against the side of another one. Yet there was no sign of any cars on the road outside. When he turned back round he noticed that Jimmy was on his feet, swaying ever so slightly.

"Sorry about that," the old man said sheepishly. "It's no fun getting old, let me tell you," he added, gently patting his stiff back. "I should get going now. But before I do, I want you to think about one more thing. Will you do that for me?"

Alfie promised he would.

"Even if your friends really do believe

that Billy is better than you, and I don't for one moment think that they really do, does it really matter? As long as you believe in yourself, that's the important thing. Is this really worth losing your friends over? After all, isn't that what Jasper would have wanted?"

Jimmy slowly shuffled towards the door. Alfie rushed over and opened it for him.

"What about, Billy?" he asked, as Jimmy passed into the hallway, before pausing to unhook his jumper. "I'd happily give up football if it would mean that we could be friends again."

"Just give Billy time," Jimmy said, almost exactly mirroring the words that Madam Zola had spoken on more than one occasion over the past few days. "Quitting football would be a huge mistake. You'd only come to regret it in time. Then you'd blame Billy for ruining your dream. You'd come to resent him. Things may seem bad at the moment, but giving up football would only make things ten times worse. Believe me. Just let him know that you're there for him, whenever he feels ready to talk."

"But how can I do that when he won't talk to me?" Alfie whined.

"I'm sure you'll think of a way, Alfie,"

the old coach said, giving the teenager a wink of encouragement.

Once they'd said their goodbyes, promising not to leave it so long before they next spoke, Alfie went upstairs to his bedroom. He pulled his phone out of his pocket and turned it on. More beeps and bings greeted him. This time, though, he didn't turn the phone straight back off. He was ready to at least read what his friends had to say for themselves. Once he had done that then he would text Daisy and arrange to meet her.

At least that was his first plan. Yet the moment he sat on his bed, ready to go through the messages, something caught his eye. Something that gave him an idea. His message to Daisy would have to wait a while longer. There was something else he needed to do first.

Five minutes later, Alfie was back outside, sprinting at top speed in the direction of his intended destination.

Friday

Chapter twenty

Jasper simply couldn't let the moment pass. For the first time in his life one of his plans had actually worked. He could hardly believe it and was determined to bask in the glory.

He had spotted them the moment he stepped foot inside the common room that break-time. Tucked away in a corner. Looking miserable.

"Morning losers," Jasper called cheerfully, as he strode cockily towards the unhappy looking trio.

There was no response from any of them.

"What? You're not going to say good morning to me?" he continued, a shark-like smile plastered on his round, red face. "I thought we were friends now. Shared secrets and everything?" he added slyly.

"Get lost," Chloe growled. Hayden and Reuben nodded but didn't say anything. They were both intimidated by the gigantic presence of their fellow pupil.

A mock expression of hurt worked its way across the larger boy's face. "But I'm so worried about you," he replied, in a tone that clearly implied that he wasn't in the slightest bit worried about them. "You all look so sad. Maybe Alfie can cheer you up. How is Alfie these days by the way? I haven't seen him for a while. Oh... wait." Jasper paused momentarily, then closed his eyes and theatrically slapped his forehead. "I forgot. You're not friends anymore, are you? How silly of me to forget."

Bravely, Chloe rose to her feet and placed herself right in front of the bully. She had to raise her head significantly to avoid staring into the boys' chest. "Just go away, Jasper, or..."

"Or what?" Jasper sneered, his tone taking on a far more menacing sound. "You'll get your two muppets here to beat me up?" He glowered meaningfully at Hayden and Reuben. The two other boys responded by averting their eyes away from Jasper's face, towards the floor. "Or are you going to do it yourself?" he continued, now looking at Chloe. "Now that would be entertaining."

For a moment, Chloe stood her ground, determined not to break eye contact with Jasper. Then, realising that she had nothing more to add, miserably slumped back down into her seat. Defeated. "Just get lost," she repeated, dejectedly.

The sound of Jasper's braying laughter cut through the three teenagers like scissors through fabric. None of them could believe they had been so stupid. Tricked by Jasper! Why had they not been more suspicious? They should have been only too aware that Jasper's concern for Billy was unlikely to have been genuine. Jasper didn't have a kind or thoughtful bone in his body. Now, not only had they lost one of their closest friends, they were being subjected to Jasper's boasts and taunts. It was unbearable.

Fortunately for them, Jasper's glee was to be short lived. For seconds later, an unexpected voice from behind immediately halted the larger boys' laughter.

"Morning guys."

Jasper spun on his heels, bewildered to be confronted by the sight of a cheerful looking Alfie, hand-in-hand with Daisy.

In fairness, Jasper wasn't the only one who looked surprised. Hayden, Reuben and Chloe all sat statue still, their mouths hanging open, as though they had seen a ghost.

"What are you doing here?" Jasper snarled.

"I've just come to talk to my friends," Alfie replied, nodding his head in the direction of the stunned trio.

"But... you don't like this lot anymore," Jasper spluttered, unable to believe what was happening. This was most definitely not part of his plan. "They all speak about you behind your back. They all think Billy's better at football than you. You heard them say it."

At once, Hayden, Chloe and Reuben all began to speak at the same time. Each one trying to explain the events that had led up to the little bits of conversation that Alfie had heard. All three were quietened by their friend's raised hand.

"I know you sent that message, Jasper," Alfie stated, looking directly at his nemesis. "And I know there was more to each of the conversations than I actually heard."

"So what!" Jasper roared, his red face beginning to go purple as anger began to surge through his veins. "They still all said that Billy's better than you. You know it's true, too. You must do. Even you're not that stupid. You're nowhere near good enough to be in an Academy. Especially if I'm not!"

Alfie smiled. He was taking great delight from Jasper's flustered response. As Daisy had suggested to him earlier that morning, this was the ideal way to get back at Jasper. Letting him know face-to-face that his plan had failed. "Maybe they were right," Alfie agreed, a confession that further stunned Jasper. "But then maybe they weren't. Maybe I'll have to work harder to prove myself. But I'm willing to do it. I'm going to do anything it takes to make it as a professional footballer. And I know that I'll stand more chance of making it if I'm surrounded by friends."

He looked pointedly at Daisy. Then at Hayden, Chloe and Reuben. All four friends responded by giving Alfie a beaming smile.

"And one thing's for sure," Alfie continued, returning his gaze to Jasper.

"I'm certainly not going to let anything you say harm my chances."

"But… but…" Jasper stuttered. He was desperately thinking of a response. Something that would put him back in control of the situation. It came to him in a flash. The second it entered his mind, his skin started to lighten and a sneer instantly replaced the scowl that had been present on his face.

"Billy," remarked the bully in a triumphant manner. "You can make friends with these muppets all you like." He gestured towards the three seated teenagers. "But Billy's your best friend. Always has been. I know that the fact he isn't talking to you hurts you more than anything. You're still not friends with him. You never will be again. Every time I've mentioned your name to him this week, I can see the hatred burning in his eyes. Being rejected by an Academy makes you bitter…"

"You'd know all about that, wouldn't you, Jasper," Alfie interrupted. He said it confidently. Not that he felt particularly confident right at that moment. Especially not when Jasper glared at him with a look that could turn fresh milk sour.

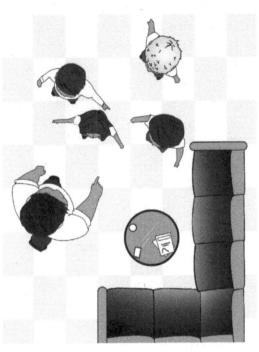

"What. Did. You. Say?" Jasper asked
through gritted teeth. His face had
turned scarlet and he'd balled his hands
so tightly into fists, that his knuckles had
turned paper-white.

Involuntarily, Alfie shut his eyes.
Certain he was about to be punched.
Hard. Fearing the same outcome,
Daisy let go of Alfie's hand and stood
protectively in front of her boyfriend.
She was instantly joined by Chloe, then,
rather more hesitantly, by Hayden and
Reuben.

Jasper took a solitary step towards the group. Nobody in the hastily formed human shield moved a muscle. Eventually, after a stand-off that lasted a good half-a-minute, Jasper took a step backwards. The tension in his previously tort body began to relax. He gave the group in front of him a wolfish grin, then shrugged his shoulders. "Whatever," he sneered. "You falling out with Billy is enough for me. You can say what you like. I know you're hurting. I win this time, losers."

With that, Jasper skulked off, groups of children scattering to allow him room to pass as he stalked angrily out of the common room.

The five friends watched him go. Once out of sight they began to talk between themselves. At first the conversation was awkward. Stilted. Reuben, Chloe and Hayden all apologised profusely for any hurt they'd caused Alfie, while Alfie was also keen to apologise for the way he had reacted. After a few moments, though, the awkwardness ceased and the group began to act as if nothing had happened. It would take more than a few sneakily recorded words to break the bonds of their friendship.

As the friends sat there joking with each other, Alfie discreetly pulled Chloe to one side.

"I just wanted to say thanks, Chloe."

"For what?" she asked, a confused expression etched on her face.

"For getting Jimmy to talk to me. He's always had a knack of getting through to me. He always seems to know what to say."

"I know," Chloe smiled. "I knew if you were going to listen to anyone it would be him."

Alfie nodded and smiled. "Anyway, thank you, for getting him to help me see sense. I don't know what I'd do without my friends."

Chloe paused for a moment. "What are you going to do about Billy?" she asked. "I know how much he means to you. As much as I hate to admit it, Jasper's right. If you don't make it up with him then Jasper really will have taken something important away from you."

Before responding, Alfie thought back to the advice he'd received from both Madam Zola and Jimmy Grimshaw over the past few days. Then to his impromptu mission the previous evening. "That's simple, Chloe," he replied confidently.

"I'm just going to give him time."

***

Ten minutes earlier, Billy had been just about to enter the common room. Then he had caught sight of Alfie and hesitated. Unsure of whether to go in or not. As he stood by the door, undecided, he noticed something odd. Alfie was deep in conversation with Jasper.

And whatever they were talking about, Jasper did not look happy. Not one bit.

Something Alfie had said had clearly annoyed the larger boy. As he watched the strange meeting through the door's glass panels, there came a moment when Billy was sure Jasper was going to hit Alfie. Part of him wanted to open the door and do something to stop the confrontation. Part of him wanted Jasper to hit him. The truth was, Billy didn't really know what he wanted anymore. Being rejected by Kingsway United had left his mind all over the place. He felt empty. Disillusioned. Alone.

He had never expected to be released. He thought he'd been doing well. Nailed on for another year. The news he had been let go had come as a complete shock.

He had only ever dreamed of being a professional footballer. Now, at just 13 years of age, he feared that dream was over. To make matters worse, Alfie, his best friend, a boy he'd always been better at football than, had been retained by his Academy. He was jealous. Extremely jealous.

Before Billy could make up his mind on what course of action to take, he stared in amazement, as Daisy, followed by Chloe, Hayden and Reuben, all placed themselves in front of Alfie. Forming a protective barrier from Jasper's wrath. He had heard through the school grapevine that Alfie had fallen out with Chloe, Hayden and Reuben, so this turn of events came as a surprise.

After what seemed like forever, Jasper backed down and eventually walked away from the group. Billy quickly moved away from the common room door, and slipped into a nearby empty classroom as Jasper stomped moodily in his direction. Then, when he was sure Jasper had gone, he silently returned to his viewing position at the door.

Seeing Alfie and the others so obviously having a good time and enjoying each other's company provoked a feeling of sadness in Billy. Would he ever feel that happy again? Could he and Alfie ever enjoy a friendship similar to that they'd once had? Billy honestly didn't know.

After spending a few more minutes watching, Billy ultimately decided against going in. Instead, he turned and headed in the direction of his next class.

On his way to the science lab, Billy swung his bag off his shoulder, opened it and pulled out a computer game. A computer game that he'd found in his porch earlier that morning. Leaning against the front door. Less than a week ago, this had been his favourite game. He played it all the time. Right now, he wasn't sure whether he ever wanted to play it again.

Billy looked at the cover. An image of a footballer wearing a yellow football shirt filled the box. Yet it wasn't this picture that his eyes were drawn to. It was at the pink post-it note that had been stuck carefully in the bottom corner. Written on the note, in handwriting he knew well, were the words:

'Bill. I'm here whenever you want to talk. No pressure. A'

Reaching his classroom moments later, the first child to arrive as break had not

169

yet quite finished, Billy looked at the box one final time. A small smile passed his lips, then disappeared. He returned the game to his bag, then lent casually against the wall waiting for class to start.

Lost deep in his own thoughts.

The following Monday

Epilogue

Alfie received the ball with his back to goal.

He spotted Liam make a great run to his right. His friend was in loads of space with no one between him and the goal. Just one simple pass, and his team would have a great chance of scoring.

Alfie, though, had no intention of passing to Liam. Instead he waited for Hayden to get closer. So close that the other boy would believe he was going to win the ball.

He could hear Liam screaming for the pass. Alfie continued to ignore him. The second he felt Hayden's leg trying to reach round for the ball, Alfie quickly placed his foot on it and feinted to drag it back one way. Hayden carefully positioned his body, ready to either make the tackle or at least block Alfie's attempted turn. Quick as a flash, Alfie swapped feet, so that his other foot was now placed on the ball. He then dragged it back the other way and gleefully spun unopposed past the completely wrongfooted Hayden.

Now he was bearing down on goal, one-on-one with the goalkeeper. Liam was still screaming for the ball. Yet Alfie knew exactly what he was going to do next. Without slowing down, he dug his left foot ever so slightly under the ball and flicked it up to knee height. Then, as the opposition goalkeeper raced off his line to claim the ball, Alfie skilfully used his knee to propel it higher into the air and over the onrushing 'keeper. He took a step right, skipped around the bemused goalie, then, without it bouncing hammered it between the two bags which formed the goal.

With ten minutes of lunchtime left, Alfie's team had taken a, surely unassailable, 11-6 lead.

"Why didn't you pass," moaned Liam. "I'm on a double hat-trick."

"Sorry Liam. I didn't see you there,"

Alfie lied. "You should have called for it."

"I was calling. Really loudly! You must have heard me?"

"Nope." Alfie smiled to himself, unable to contain his laughter as Liam confirmed with other teammates that he had indeed been calling for the pass.

He was pleased that Reuben had suggested playing another lunchtime match. While he truly loved training and playing in matches for Norton Town, he often missed the freedom he got from a kickabout with his friends. There was something enjoyable about being temporarily away from the pressure and structure of Academy football.

"I definitely called," Liam sulked as he walked over to Alfie. "And anyway. Did you really have to hit it so hard? The ball's gone miles."

In fairness, Liam had a point. Alfie was so close to the goal that he could have hit it with a quarter of the power and still scored. Yet he'd got lost in the moment. Carried away by the fun of it all and so ended up smashing it into the distance.

"It's alright. I'll get it," Alfie chuckled as he sped off in pursuit of the ball, which had rolled down a bank.

Slowing down as he approached the

slope, so as not to embarrassingly tumble down it, Alfie scanned left and right to see where it had actually rolled to. He couldn't spot it anywhere. Confused, he did a quick circuit of the picnic area located at the bottom of the bank. There was no ball to be found.

He was just about to go back and reluctantly admit that he had lost the ball, when someone tapped him on the shoulder.

"Looking for this?"

Alfie twisted to face the person who had spoken. He was unable to supress his delight at the sight of Billy holding the ball out to him.

He nodded, took the offered ball and thanked Billy. Yet before he could say anything further, the other boy had turned back around and was already walking steadily in the opposite direction.

Alfie watched him go for a while, cursing under his breath that he hadn't said anything further.

Seconds later, he heard someone from the field, it sounded like Liam, shout to ask where he had gotten to. Shaking his disappointment aside, he was about to turn and head back to the field when he noticed that Billy had stopped walking.

Time seemed to slow. The other boy turned around and looked directly at Alfie. With his next four words he gave Alfie hope that maybe, just maybe, everything would be alright.

"Can I join in?"

Turn the page to read
the first two chapters
of **Split Loyalties**
- a Kindle only book
written by David Fuller.

Download your copy
today...

Hugh

Hugh Capulet had been completely
obsessed with football for as long as he
– or anyone else for that matter – could
remember.

From the very moment that Hugh had
taken his first unsteady steps at just over
ten-months old, a ball had rarely been far
from his feet.

As a baby, he would simply refuse point
blank to fall asleep unless a football
was placed in his cot, while few, if any,
childhood photos of Hugh exist in which
he's not either kicking or dribbling a ball.

In fact, there's probably more chance of
seeing a photo of the Loch Ness Monster
and Bigfoot sitting together whilst
enjoying a quiet cup of tea on the lawns
of Buckingham Palace, than there is of

seeing a picture of an adolescent Hugh without a ball somewhere near his feet.

Given the extent of his obsession, it's probably not all that surprising to learn that Hugh began to exhibit a talent for the sport before he was even out of nappies. He was as comfortable dribbling a football as most babies are dribbling their dinner down their clothes.

By the age of nine, Hugh had been selected for League One Portland Town's Academy team. He signed his first professional contract with the same club on his seventeenth birthday, having won the team's player of the year award every single season since first joining the academy.

It didn't take long for Premier League scouts to recognise Hugh's obvious potential. While he was still a teenager he signed his first multi-million pound contract with the newly-crowned league champions, Lexington Albion – England's most successful ever football team.

Since then, a raft of individual and team honours had come his way and he had even become a regular for the Italian national team.

Yet, in spite of all the trophies that he'd won, the fan adulation he'd received, and the massive amounts of money he had earned in the seven years since first signing for Lexington, it was still a love of football, rather than any other associated reward, that made him tick.

Each and every time he stepped onto a pitch, he still received the exact same buzz that he'd experienced before playing his very first match as a six year old for the Ashgate Athletic under 7s.

His heart beat would start to race and a nervous shiver of excitement would run down the entire length of his spine, before an involuntary beaming smile would break out across his face.

For years he had tended to be the first player to arrive at Lexington's luxurious Middleton training complex every single day, and more often than not he would be the last to leave, too.

And when he wasn't playing in a match or at training, the chances were that he was either watching a match on the TV, or playing one of his many football-related console games.

Yes, it's fair to say that Hugh Capulet had been completely obsessed with football for a very, very long time.

Until now.

There was just one day remaining

before Hugh was due to meet up with his Italian teammates ahead of boarding a plane to travel to Brazil for the World Cup and Hugh should have been buzzing with excitement. This was due to be his first major international tournament, having picked up a tournament-ending knee injury on the eve of the European Championships two years earlier.

Feeling fit and healthy, and having just had the best season of his career with Lexington, he should have been as excited as a hyperactive four-year-old on Christmas Eve at the prospect of representing his beloved Italia in the biggest football tournament of all.

Instead he was dreading it.

And it was all his family's fault.

Family ties

There's little doubt that Hugh's devotion
to football was passed on to him by his
Italian grandparents from his father's
side of the family.

From the moment he was born, *Nonno*
(grandpa) and *Nona* (grandma) Capulet
had simply doted on baby Hugh, and had
insisted almost instantly upon looking
after him full-time during the week, so
that his Mum could go back to work –
even though she hadn't really wanted to.

Rather than letting him watch cartoons
and play with cuddly toys, like most
infants, *Nonno* and *Nona* instead only let
their beloved grandson play with balls,
while football on the television formed
a near constant backdrop to Hugh's
formative years.

Not that he seemed to mind.

By the time of his first birthday, Hugh had little interest in anything that wasn't round and didn't roll, while the only way his parents were able to soothe his regular screaming fits was by putting football on the TV. No sooner did Hugh hear the commentator's soothing voice or the roar of the crowd, did his tantrums subside and he quickly became the most docile baby there ever was.

The love that Hugh held for his Italian grandparents was clear for all to see... much to the annoyance of his English grandparents on his mother's side of the family.

Nana and Gramps Sampson quickly became jealous of the amount of time that their grandson spent with the Italian side of the family; a jealously that only increased once Hugh learned to speak and then spent practically the whole time talking about *Nonno* and *Nona*... and football, of course.

Therefore, when Hugh's brother Monty was born just over four years after him, Nana and Gramps made sure that this time it would be they who would be the ones to look after the newborn – once again practically forcing the boy's poor mother into a far earlier than planned return to work.

In the years that followed, tensions between the Sampson and Capulet grandparents intensified. Just as Nana and Gramps had resented the amount of time that *Nonno* and *Nona* had spent with Hugh, so too did the Italian grandparents start to begrudge Monty being hogged by the English relatives.

Family gatherings soon started to resemble battle grounds rather than the happy occasions they should have been, as both sets of grandparents constantly competed for the attention of their grandchildren. It was as if they felt a prize would be awarded for buying the best – or more likely most expensive – present.

Such gatherings would often see both sets of grandparents boasting of exactly how much they'd spent on the children, and on more than one occasion the day had ended with *Nonno*, *Nona*, Nana and Gramps all sat around the dining-room table angrily comparing receipts.

As the years rolled by, the situation became so bad that Hugh and Monty's parents decided to do everything they could to keep the two sides of the family separate at all time. Naturally, by request, Hugh still tended to spend more time with Nonno and Nona than Monty, while the younger Capulet continued to see more of Nana and Gramps.

However, in spite of the ongoing rivalry between the Italian and English members of Hugh and Monty's extended family, the love that the two brothers held for each other was, and always had been, clear for all to see.

Yet it was a combination of the love that Hugh felt for Monty and the disdain that the English and Italian grandparents had for each other, that was now threatening to extinguish Hugh's passion for football and ruin his World Cup dream.

Visit the Kindle store today to read the rest of Split Loyalties